BREATHING BOOKS

30878 4113
R

Copyright © 2018 by Cornelia Funke
English translation copyright © 2018 by Cornelia Funke

Second Edition: March 2018

10 9 8 7 6 5 4 3 2 1

Book design by Mirada
Printed in Canada

THE WILD CHICKS

CORNELIA FUNKE

PREFACE

I am often asked whether I base my stories on my own life. "Well," I mostly answer, "I usually don't ride dragons or step through magical mirrors. But there is this series, which caused thousands of German girls to walk around with feathers around their necks, build tree houses and chicken coops and…look for boys they could call the Pygmies. One of its characters is based on the mean grandmother of my mother, and I used everything I know about growing up in 1980s Germany for these books: about loving parents, bad parents, jealousy and friendship and…chickens of course!"

I love to write fantasy, so why did I ever write girls' books (which I never read when I was young)? Because one day my editor said: "Cornelia, would you write a book without dragons or fairies for a change?"

"Why?" I responded. "That would be terribly boring."

"Please try. Just one," she said.

So I sat down, and the Wild Chicks were born. Soon I got letters like: "Please Cornelia! Make the world a better place! Write another Wild Chicks book!" or "When I get sad, I just have to touch the Wild Chicks book I keep under my pillow." Those letters were so irresistible that I wrote another and another and another…eventually, they were turned into movies in Germany and, when I do events, young German women come up to me and whisper: "I was a Wild Chick. Thank you!"

I wonder what American girls will think of these books — there are no mobile phones, and the heroines are done with school by 2pm at the latest. They are all Northern German by descent, which was the reality of the small suburban towns I grew up in during the eighties, but luckily I've learned that most readers find something of themselves in one — or all! — of the girls, no matter their background, race, or sexuality, which is once again proof that we are all not that different. If my stories remind some readers of that truth, my job as a writer is done.

So…please let me know how you like my girls. And the boys of course. A boy once said in a reading. "Thank you, Cornelia! One can learn everything about girls reading *The Wild Chicks*." I admit that was never my intention, but books do have a way of telling the stories they want to tell.

With love to all the wild girls in the world,

CHAPTER I

It was a wonderful day, as warm and fluffy as chicken feathers. Sadly, it was also a Monday, and the huge clock above the school entrance already showed a quarter past eight as Charlie came speeding into the school yard.

"Blast!" she muttered as she shoved her bike into the rusty bike stand and yanked her school bag from the basket. She stormed up the stairs and ran through the empty assembly hall.

On the stairs she nearly ran over Mr. Mouseman, the janitor.

"Whoa!" he spluttered, nearly choking on his cheese sandwich.

"I'm sorry!" Charlie muttered as she stormed on. Two more corridors and then she stood, panting, in front of her classroom door. Behind the door there was deadly silence, as always when Mrs. Rose was holding class. Charlie took one more gasp of air, then knocked and opened the door.

"Sorry, Mrs. Rose," she mumbled. "I had to feed the chickens."

Big Steve stared at her, stunned. Pretty Melanie arched her eyebrows. And Fred, ever the joker, flapped his arms and crowed. Very funny.

"Well, that's an original excuse for a change," Mrs. Rose said, pouting her red lips as she made a mark in her little notebook.

Glum-faced, Charlie went to her seat. She poked her tongue out at Fred and sat down next to Freya, her very best friend.

"You've got straw in your hair," Freya whispered. "Why did you have to feed the chickens? Is Grandma Stalberg sick?"

Charlie shook her head and yawned. "Gone to her sister's. And now I have to get up an hour earlier every day to feed the chickens. One hour! Can you imagine?"

"That's quite enough with the whispering back there," Mrs. Rose called as she began to draw mysterious numbers on the blackboard. Freya and Charlie ducked their heads until their noses nearly touched their books.

"But at least I had an idea!" Charlie whispered.

"Yeah?" Freya looked worried. Charlie's ideas were generally worse than the measles. And she constantly kept hatching out new ones.

"Send a message to Trudie and Melanie!" Charlie hissed out of the corner of her mouth. "Secret meeting, next recess, girls' toilets."

Trudie and Melanie sat next to each other, three rows ahead. They were both studiously staring at the blackboard.

"Oh no!" Freya moaned. "You're not starting with that

gang-stuff again?"

"Write!" Charlie hissed.

Freya had mastered the secret gang code perfectly, something that could definitely not be said about Charlie, even though she had invented it. No surprises there—she couldn't even remember whether to write 'teacher' with 'ee' or 'ea'.

"Right! Can I have someone at the blackboard, please?" Mrs. Rose announced.

Freya ducked her head again. Charlie stared intently at her textbook.

"No volunteers?"

"Password?" Freya whispered, tearing a page from her notebook.

Charlie scrawled something on the table top.

Freya screwed up her face. "What's that supposed to mean?"

"It's a chicken, duh!" Charlie hissed angrily. "And it's an excellent password, okay? Hurry up!"

Mrs. Rose was again looking in their direction.

"Fred's volunteering!" Charlie called out. She erased the misshapen chicken with her thumb.

"Haha!" Fred slid deeper into his chair.

"Done!" Freya carefully folded the message and slid it across the table toward Charlie.

"Charlotte, how about you?" Mrs. Rose.

"Oh no, please, there's really no point," Charlie replied. "Really, there isn't, Mrs. Rose."

"Charlotte? To the front. *Please!*" Mrs. Rose's eyebrows were slowly rising. They always did that when she got angry.

Charlie got up. She snatched the note from her table and dropped it into Melanie's lap. But hidden behind Mrs. Rose's round glasses were a set of eagle-sharp eyes. "Melanie? Could you show me that piece of paper you just received?" she chirped. Pretty Melanie's face turned crimson-red and she brought Charlie's secret message to the front.

"*Nekcih cdrowe docsse certxe noolsl rigeht nognit eem,*" Mrs. Rose read aloud. "What's this?"

"That's Charlie's stupid secret code," Fred announced. He was grinning so madly that his ears were threatening to fall off. Charlie took a piece of chalk and stared at the blackboard, her lips tightly squeezed together.

"Well, if it's secret," Mrs. Rose folded Charlie's message and dropped it back into Melanie's hand, "Then it should remain secret. Charlotte, please begin."

The remainder of the period was quite unpleasant for Charlie. But at least Fred was also racking his brains, about 'Nekcih cdrowe' and so on.

"This is a stupid place to meet!" Melanie declared. Three of them were squeezed into a single toilet cubicle. Freya had gotten the best spot. She was sitting on the lid.

"This is the only place where Fred's gang can't spy on us," Charlie retorted.

"Spy on us? What's there to spy on?" Melanie jeered. She was fluffing up her blonde curls. "I'm sure the boys have better things to do."

"Really?"

Someone knocked on the cubicle door and whispered, "Chicken! Chiiiickeeen!"

Charlie unlocked the door, and Trudie squeezed in to join them—things were getting seriously cramped.

"Sorry," Trudie mumbled sheepishly, "But I had to go to the loo. I mean, for real." She blushed. "So what's up?"

"Charlie has an idea," Freya said.

Melanie plopped a chewing gum between her bright white teeth. "Well, if it's anything like the last one, count me out."

"If our gang is such a drag, then why are you here?" Charlie hissed at her.

Melanie narrowed her eyes. "Fine! Spit it out, your *idea*." She giggled and gave Trudie a nudge. "Maybe she wants to cook another witch's potion—turn our faces green for days."

Charlie replied with an icy stare.

"Jeez, do you think we could finally get to the point?" Freya asked. She climbed onto the toilet lid and opened the window.

"All right." Charlie rubbed her nose. She always did that when she was angry, or embarrassed. "My gran's gone for a week to visit her sister, who is even more ancient than her. I'm looking after the house and the chickens and all that. So, I thought that would make an excellent gang headquarters, and if we meet a few times this week, well, we could maybe get to be a real gang."

"I like it," Trudie said with a sideways glance at Melanie. For her, something was only ever really okay once Melanie had agreed to it, but her friend wasn't looking at all convinced.

"What do you mean, a few times?" Melanie asked.

"I…maybe…every day?"

Freya shook her head. "Oh, I'm not sure I can make it that often. You know, my little brother…"

"God, your little brother," Charlie muttered angrily. "Why can't your big brother look after him for a change?"

"You can talk," Freya mumbled. Charlie had no brothers or sisters. Her mother drove a taxi, so she was hardly ever around. And her father, well, he wasn't around at all, and it was best not to mention him. Ever.

"And what are we going to do with ourselves?" Melanie asked.

"And what exciting stuff do you usually get up to?" Charlie asked angrily. "Me, I just sit around at home, unless I'm slaving away at my gran's. Freya does nothing but look after her little brother. And Trudie's also not having one mega-adventure after another, as far as I know, right?"

Trudie smiled in embarrassment at the dirty tiles in front

of her feet.

"I have ballet," Melanie replied tartly. "And I have guitar lessons."

"Sounds really exciting!" Charlie mocked her. "I'm sure you can miss those for one week."

"Of course I can!" Melanie's eyes narrowed with anger. "But then what?"

"Well…we'll see!" Charlie yelled. "You can't plan an adventure like some ballet lesson or something. They're just there, lurking, right around some corner, and then, suddenly—wham!—they happen."

The three others looked at each other. Their heads were suddenly filled with treasure, knights, and pirates. Charlie had done it again.

Trudie gave Melanie a tentative smile. "I'd like to give it a try," she said.

Melanie shrugged. "Fine. One week. Then we'll see."

Trudie beamed at her with relief.

"I'm in," Freya said. "I just might have to bring my brother."

"Good!" Charlie took a deep breath. "So we meet this afternoon, around three. Agreed?"

"Fine by me," said Melanie. "But I'm not putting on that stupid gang t-shirt again. It's not flattering."

"But we have to have something we all wear!" Charlie replied angrily. "And I definitely won't get into some frilly dress just to make you look good."

"Gang uniform is boring anyway," Freya said. "How about a tattoo or something?"

Trudie just stared at her.

"Just an idea," Freya muttered.

"Maybe we can come up with something," Charlie said. "Three o'clock. And don't forget the password."

"Chiiihiiicken!" Melanie warbled, screwing her eyes. "And now can someone explain to me why we had to discuss this in the bathroom?"

CHAPTER 2

Charlie and Freya lived in the same street, which is quite a handy thing when you're best friends. They'd known each other since kindergarten, had fallen out forever at least a hundred times, and had made up just as often—as best friends do. Once they even ran away together—all the way to the next street corner.

At two-thirty sharp, Charlie picked up Freya to go to her gran's. Freya was pushing a stroller, as she had to look after her little brother Luke again.

"A baby on a gang meet!" Charlie shook her head. "We're never going to be a proper gang!"

Swoosh! The pacifier flew out of the stroller.

"Oh no!" Freya quickly snatched it from underneath a Chihuahua peeing against a newspaper stand.

"Can't your big brother look after the baby for a change?" Charlie asked.

"Nope," Freya carefully wiped the pacifier on her t-shirt. "He's got tennis."

"Right. And last time it was what? Karate?"

And the pacifier went flying again—this time in a particularly high trajectory. "Karate is Wednesdays," Freya said. "Damn, where did that thing land now?"

Luke started screaming.

"Probably landed on the road and got flattened," Charlie told Freya impatiently. "Haven't you got another one? He screams louder than all the cars together."

Freya quickly pulled a reserve pacifier from her pocket and stuffed it into the greedy little mouth. When Luke had just been born, Charlie called him *sugarbear*, but by now her enthusiasm for the baby had waned considerably. Freya felt the same.

They turned into a narrow street. After only a few steps, the noise of the traffic faded to a low rumble, and they could hear the wheels of the stroller crunching on the gravel.

"So what do the boys do in their gang?" Freya asked.

"They go fishing," Charlie replied. "And they annoy girls. That's all their birdbrains can come up with."

"What about us?" Freya asked. "Have you had any ideas? Maybe we could cook together, or something. Melanie would probably like that, too."

"Here we go again: Melanie, Melanie. She can go off to her ballet lessons if she starts whining again!" Charlie screamed. And Luke immediately started howling.

"Keep it down!" Freya hissed. She quickly rocked the stroller until the baby quieted down again.

"I'm sorry," Charlie whispered. "It just gets to me how Trudie worships her, and now you, too. Anyway, cooking's not for gangs."

"It was just an idea," Freya replied. "Why did you let Melanie in the gang in the first place if you hate her so much?"

"There was nobody better around," Charlie muttered, rubbing her nose. "And it was you who suggested her, didn't you?"

"I suggested Trudie because she's always over at our place." Trudie's and Freya's mums were very good friends.

Charlie sighed. "And Trudie won't do anything without Melanie."

"Exactly."

Charlie hadn't suggested anyone. Who could she have suggested, anyway? Freya was not only her best friend, she was her only friend.

"Doesn't matter," Charlie continued. "A gang is a gang, and those two aren't all bad. You'll see, this is going to be a great week. Definitely."

"Sure. Of course." Freya replied. She didn't sound very convinced. "Could you have a peek in the stroller?"

"Sleeping." Charlie observed. "Babies are quite cute when they sleep, but when they're not—phew!"

Charlie's gran lived in a narrow street with meadows on one side and a row of old houses on the other. The houses were neither big nor pretty, but they all had proper gardens.

Freya had only been there once before, and that had been

enough. Grandma Stalberg did not like it when Charlie brought friends over. "I do not like strangers in my house," she would say. And to her everybody was a stranger, except for Charlie and her mother. Grandma Stalberg was quite strange. She kept forgetting things, and she loved bossing people around. After Freya had met her, she had suddenly understood why Charlie was so sad so often, and why she could be so nasty to others, sometimes even to her best friend.

When Charlie's mum was out driving her taxi, Charlie would eat at her gran's, and when her mother drove the night shift Charlie had to sleep over. After lunch, she'd have to weed for hours, or clean out the chicken coop, for Grandma Stalberg was of the firm opinion that children had to earn their keep. "By the sweat of their brow," she would say. "Yes, sir, by the sweat of their brow."

And so Charlie was very knowledgeable about vegetable gardens and chicken coops—and nasty grans.

Grandma Stalberg's house was the last one in the street—a gloomy brick house with tiny windows that looked like squinting eyes. There wasn't a patch of grass anywhere in the large garden, nor was there a terrace, and flowers were very scarce. But there were countless berry-bushes and fruit trees, as well as long rows of tidy vegetable patches. At the back there was an old shed and a green henhouse, with a large run and a chain-link fence around it.

"Oh, the hens!" Freya called out as they stopped in front of Grandma Stalberg's gate. "Are there any new ones?"

Charlie shook her head. "Nope, there's actually one less. Gran slaughtered one last week, to take to her sister." Charlie's desperate pleas and even her tears had done nothing to stop her gran. But at least she had spared Charlie's favorite hen.

"Oh, blast!" Charlie suddenly called out. She yanked the gate open and ran toward the vegetable patches. "Get away! Shoo!" she screamed.

A fat brown hen peered out from between the cabbages, a large leaf still hanging from her beak. When she saw Charlie angrily charging toward her, she quickly fluttered toward the coop, clucking loudly.

"Just you wait!" Charlie yelled. She tried to grab the hen, but the big bird cackled hysterically and ran up and down the fence. Charlie tried to grab her twice. Feathers were flying. Then the hen suddenly ducked her head and slipped underneath the green gate, into the run.

Freya nearly choked laughing.

"Stop giggling, you jerk!" Charlie ran back to the cabbage patch with a worried frown. Two of the heads had been reduced to stumps. Charlie angrily pulled them out of the ground and threw them into the chicken run. Freya pushed the baby's stroller toward the house. She was still snickering.

"It's not funny!" Charlie whined. "I'm going to be in big

trouble when my gran sees this."

"Come on, can't be that bad," Freya replied sheepishly.
"Oops! Now I've got a hiccup."

"Those stupid birds keep digging under the gate!" Charlie
sighed. "I fill up the hole and the very next day they dig a new
one. Try explaining that to my gran!"

"Calm down!" Freya put her arm around Charlie's
shoulder. "If she's as forgetful as you always say, then she'll
have no idea how many cabbages she had in that patch." She
peered into the stroller. "Luke's sleeping like a log. I'll just
leave him out here."

Charlie still looked quite desperate. "My gran never
forgets about that sort of thing," she said. "She'd forget her
own name first. She even knows how many rusty nails she's
got in the jar in the shed." Glum-faced, Charlie pulled the
key from her pocket. There were three gleaming security locks
on Grandma Stalberg's rickety front door. Amazed, Freya
shook her head.

"Has your gran got some sort of treasure in there?"

"Not as far as I know," Charlie grumbled. She fiddled
exasperatedly with the keys. "My gran keeps seeing burglars
behind every head of cabbage. There's nothing to steal in here.
Come on in." She pushed the door open.

They walked through a small hallway with a huge
wardrobe and entered Grandma Stalberg's kitchen. It was
a beautiful kitchen. There was an old cupboard with lots of

drawers and glass doors, and a big table with three chairs and a sofa.

"Looks cozy," Freya commented.

But Charlie frowned. "Just look at that!" she muttered angrily. She walked over to the cupboard and pulled off a note that had been taped to the glass door. "Monday and Wednesday: wipe floors," she read. "Charming, isn't she?"

There were more notes, and they were everywhere: on the oven, on the fridge, on the door to the larder, on the table. Sometimes there were two notes in the same place. All of them contained exact instructions. Charlie tore them all down. Her face had grown bright red.

Freya took the pile of paper from her friend's hand and started to read. 'Feed the chickens' – 'clean the coop' – 'weed the vegetable patches' ("And do it properly this time!") – 'air the house' – 'change the table cloth' – dust here, sweep there, wipe that…finally, Freya had enough, and she threw the whole pile on the table.

There was one more note taped to the table top. This one had a large bunch of keys next to it.

Red: Key to the larder – fingers off the biscuits.

Blue: Shed. Make sure there's always fresh bacon in the mousetraps.

Yellow: Spare keys for front door—just in case you 'mislay' yours again. Wouldn't be the first time!

Green: Mailbox. Empty <u>daily!</u>

Black: None of your business!

"What's that supposed to mean?" Freya asked perplexed. "Maybe she has a treasure hidden here somewhere after all! What do you think?"

Charlie shook her head. "No idea. Weird." She looked pensively at the black key. It didn't look any different from the others.

"Hey, Charlie! Are you here?" someone called outside— and Luke immediately started screaming.

"Hi! Your baby's crying!" Melanie said as she sauntered into the kitchen with Trudie in tow.

"No wonder, with the noise you're making," Freya said. She went out and returned with the screaming baby. "He's soaking wet. I've got to clean him up. Can someone put his blanket on the table?"

Trudie shot out of the kitchen like lightning and brought the blanket from the stroller. Charlie was still standing there, staring at the black key.

"Out of my way!" Freya muttered. She freed Luke from his soaked diaper. Trudie was mesmerized.

"What's so interesting about that key?" Melanie asked.

"That's what I'd like to know!" Charlie mumbled. Then she stuffed the bunch of keys and the pile of rude instructions into her pocket.

CHAPTER 3

"**T**here are no roosters!" Melanie observed.

The four girls were sitting in the middle of the chicken run, around a rickety table laid out with tea and biscuits.

"Roosters just cause trouble," Charlie explained. The hens were under the table squabbling over crumbs. Charlie grabbed a small black hen and put her on her lap. She gently stroked her comb and the hen closed her eyes.

Melanie giggled. "Aren't you afraid she might poo on your lap?"

"Nope—and I'm not as tarted up as you, anyway," Charlie replied. Melanie pursed her lips and brushed the crumbs from her dress.

"Do they all have names?" Trudie asked.

Charlie nodded. "Sure. This one is Emma. Down there are Isolde, Huberta, the checkered one is called Kokoschka, and those two fat ones there are Dolly and Clara."

"Nice names," Melanie said. "Did your gran come up with them?"

Charlie shook her head. "No, I named them all. And our gang should also have a name, don't you think?"

"Fred's gang has a great name," Freya said. Luke was on

her lap, dry and happy, and sucking on her finger.

"The *Pygmies*!" Charlie screwed her eyes. "You think that's great? I don't know."

"And they all have earrings." Trudie shoveled four spoons of sugar into her tea. "They all got into massive trouble with their parents for that." Her admiration was obvious.

"How about…" Melanie took another one of Grandma Stalberg's forbidden biscuits, "…we call ourselves the Fairies? Sounds great, I think."

"Over my dead body!" Charlie took the kicking Emma from her lap and put her back under the table. Trudie was reaching for the cookie-jar, but Charlie pushed her hand away and snapped the lid shut. "That's enough, or else my gran will know I couldn't have eaten them all by myself."

"Oh." Embarrassed, Trudie folded her hands in her lap.

"So what's your favorite name, Charlie?" Melanie asked pertly.

"The *Wild Chicks*," Charlie answered. "That would be a good name."

Melanie's angel face screwed up in disgust. Trudie and Freya, however, nodded.

"Sounds fun, Freya said. "Yes, definitely sounds fun."

"And as a gang tag," Trudie was excitedly shifting in her chair, "We could all paint our fingernails green."

"No, our toenails!" Freya chimed in. "Or our lips!"

"Yuck!" Charlie moaned. "Then we might as well all dye

our hair."

"No way!" Melanie shrieked. She was polishing her shoe with a napkin. "If you really want to call yourselves the *Wild Chicks*, fine. But I will not dye my hair."

"I know!" Trudie blew her fringe out of her eyes. "We all wear a chicken feather around our neck. And we can never lose it, or have anyone take it from us, or else…"

"Hmm!" Charlie was thinking.

Melanie's pretty nose crinkled up. "Ugh! We'll all smell like chicken poo!"

"No we won't!" Charlie picked a feather from the ground and held it under Melanie's nose. "Can your perfect nose smell anything? See?" She looked around. "Everybody pick one. Plenty here to choose from."

The chickens looked even more puzzled than usual as the four girls started darting around the run, their eyes firmly on the ground. It took quite a while until each *Wild Chick* was sure she had found the prettiest feather.

"I'll put mine on a silver necklace," Melanie announced. "It'll look quite pretty."

"Sure!" Trudie looked admiringly at her friend. Freya and Charlie exchanged a look.

"And now for the most important thing," Charlie said, "Which none of you have thought about…"

The others looked at her expectantly.

Charlie made a very important face. "The oath!"

"What?" Freya asked. "Why?"

"She's right!" Trudie said. "The oath is very important." She fished a crumpled chocolate bar from her pocket devoured it in one bite.

"Like, with blood and stuff?" Freya shook her head angrily. "I won't do that." Luke was kicking around, pointing his stubby fingers at the hens. Then he started screaming. Freya got up with a sigh and started walking up and down with him. Trudie tossed her empty chocolate wrapper onto the ground. The hens jumped on it greedily, but quickly dropped it again in disappointment.

"We could just prick our fingers," Charlie suggested.

Trudie's face grew quite pale as she quickly hid her chocolate-stained fingers in her lap.

"And then we all get blood poisoning or something. No, thank you," Melanie declared. "We'll use spit. Spit works just as well."

"Spit?" Charlie shrugged. "All right then. So we all spit on our fingers and then we rub them together."

"But first Trudie has to clean her hands!" Melanie said. "She looks like she's eaten dog poo."

Trudie's face went as red as a chicken comb. She quickly rubbed her hands on her trousers.

"Right!" Charlie looked at the others. "Everybody get up and repeat after me: I swear to protect the secrets of the *Wild Chicks* with my life, never to tell anybody anything, or else I will drop dead on the spot."

"We swear!" the other three chimed in. Then they all rubbed their spittle-fingers together. The hens rocked their heads and clucked nervously.

"And what are our secrets?" Melanie dropped back into her chair and carefully wiped her finger on the tablecloth.

"Our gang mark, our codeword, our secret code—and all that," Charlie explained.

"That's it?"

"Well," Charlie gave them all a meaningful look. "There's something else I'm looking into, but I'll tell you about that tomorrow."

And again the other three had the feeling that adventure was already lurking behind the chain link fence, and that the world was wild and exciting. *It's her voice*, Freya thought. Charlie's voice was always a little raspy, and it felt as if she could brush your skin with it like sandpaper.

"Come on, don't get all mysterious on us now," Melanie said. She was always the first to break free of Charlie's spell.

But Charlie shook her head. "Tomorrow."

"Fine! I have to go home now anyway," Freya said. "Luke is getting hungry." She quickly ran to the stroller.

"All right." Melanie and Trudie got up as well. "Yuck!" Melanie stared in shock at her shoes. "One of those nasty chickens just shat on my shoes!"

"They always pick the fanciest ones!" Charlie giggled.

Melanie spun around and stormed off. "See you tomorrow, then. Trudie, come!"

"See you tomorrow." Trudie quickly ran after Melanie.

Freya was already by the gate, looking for Luke's pacifier again. "Aren't you coming?" she shouted over the fence at Charlie. Luke was screaming like crazy.

Charlie shook her head. "I'll stay here for a while. Mum's still driving anyway."

Freya had found the pacifier under the hedge. It had an old candy wrapper stuck to it.

"Right, then," she said. "See you tomorrow. Take care." And off she went with the stroller and her screaming brother.

"Tomorrow," Charlie mumbled. She put the cups and the cold tea on a tray and shook out the tablecloth before carefully checking it for stains. At least half of it was covered with chocolate fingers. *Blast. Why did Trudie have to eat constantly?* Charlie quickly took the tablecloth to the house to soak it. Then she took the table and the chairs back to the shed and looked around the garden. No. Not even Grandma Stalberg's sharp eyes would have spotted any signs of the *Wild Chicks'* first gang meet.

Charlie took a handful of chicken feed and sat down on an overturned bucket in the middle of the chicken run. The hens quickly came waddling toward her. They pecked at Charlie's fingers, tucked at her shoelaces, and winked at her with their bright button eyes.

Charlie had to laugh. Chickens really were too funny. She took the key and her grandmother's note from her pocket and looked at them thoughtfully. The hens peered at her curiously and pecked at the piece of paper.

"Weird," Charlie muttered, turning the black key in her hands. "Really weird."

Then she fetched three eggs from the coop and pulled a few potatoes from the ground. *Time to make some dinner.*

CHAPTER 4

The next afternoon Freya was off baby duty, and they also had hardly any homework. Ideal conditions for a wonderful gang meeting.

At three o'clock sharp they all sat around Grandma Stalberg's kitchen table, waiting nervously for Charlie to reveal her secret. The sun was shining through the open window, a magpie was chattering somewhere, and the bees were humming in the lime tree by the house.

Charlie cleared her throat and looked at their eager faces. She held her silence for a few more seconds, for maximum effect.

"Just spit it out!" Melanie burst out impatiently.

"Yes, please!" Trudie chimed in with her mouth full. She was munching through a huge sausage roll.

"Shall I make some tea?" Charlie asked.

"No!" Freya said, grinning. "Just tell us already!"

Charlie reached into her pocket and produced Grandma Stalberg's key and the note. With a solemn expression, she put both on the table. Then she read a slightly condensed version of the note.

"Quite a nice grandma you have there," Melanie observed after Charlie had finished.

"The secret is about the black key, isn't it?" Trudie asked

with a muted voice. The excitement made her eyes as round as coat buttons. For a few moments she even forgot about her roll.

"Last night, after you all left, I tried all the locks I could find," Charlie told them. "Nothing."

"You think your gran has a treasure hidden here somewhere?" Trudie whispered.

"Oh Trudie, why are you whispering like that?" Melanie asked. "Do you think Charlie's gran is hiding in the wardrobe or something?"

Trudie bit her lip and blushed.

"It's probably not a treasure, but a horribly rotten corpse," said Freya. "Did your grandpa vanish suddenly?"

"Rubbish!" Charlie shook her head angrily.

"Well, the way I read this note," Melanie giggled, "I'd expect all sorts of nasty stuff from your grandma."

Outside, one of the hens started clucking madly. Charlie looked at the window and frowned.

"Why do you think she's making such a secret of the key?" Freya asked. The day before, she'd racked her brains over it all the way home, but the only result was that it had made her even more freaked out by Charlie's grandma.

"Maybe it's just for a drawer where your gran keeps her secret cookie recipes," Melanie suggested. Charlie was still staring at the window. Suddenly she got up and carefully walked toward it. Freya looked at her quizzically. "Hey, what…?"

Charlie put a warning finger on her lips.

"So, maybe there's nothing mysterious at all about that key!" Melanie said loudly. She had also gotten up and was now tiptoeing toward the front door.

"Nah, definitely not!" Freya agreed, now also sneaking up to the window. Only Trudie was still sitting at the table, her mouth open and her half-eaten roll in her hand.

Then Charlie suddenly screamed out: "Stop, you filthy spies!" And with that she jumped in one leap out of the window. Freya followed, not quite as quickly on her short legs. Melanie tore open the front door and ran outside.

Now Trudie finally shook herself out of her stupor. She struggled off of the sofa and stumbled to the window, just in time to see Fred, Baz, Steve, and Willie—the entire *Pygmies* gang—dash off across Grandma Stalberg's vegetable beds. Charlie, Freya, and Melanie were hot on their heels. They had nearly caught up with them when Charlie suddenly screamed and pointed at the chicken run.

The gate was wide open. And the run was deserted.

That short moment of shock saved the *Pygmies*. They climbed over the garden gate, grabbed their bicycles, and sped off.

"All gone!" Charlie muttered. Her lower lip was trembling a little. Perplexed, she looked around, but the hens had vanished.

Trudie, panting heavily, caught up with them. She stared

at the empty pen. "Maybe they're inside the henhouse!" she suggested.

Charlie shook her head.

"That's so mean!" Freya moaned. "So bloody mean!"

"Come." Melanie took Charlie by the arm. "Where's the feed? Maybe we can lure them back."

"I see one, by the cabbages!" Freya called out. "It's the speckled one."

"Watch that she doesn't run away!" Charlie shouted. "We'll get the feed."

"How am I supposed to do that?" Freya shouted back. But the others had already vanished into the shed, and she carefully snuck around the hen so she could at least block her path to the gate. The hen's head shot up and her little eyes blinked nervously at the girl.

"It's aaaall-riiiight, staaaay caaaaalm," Freya hummed.

The hen clucked quietly.

The other three came back out of the shed. Melanie and Trudie had chicken feed in their hands. The hen turned nervously toward them, though she still took one more peck at the head of cabbage in front of her.

"Come on, Kokoschka, come!" Charlie said soothingly as she slowly came closer. Melanie threw some feed on the ground in front of Charlie's feet.

"We have to encircle her," Charlie hissed. They spread out. Kokoschka craned her neck with interest.

"Crouch down!" Charlie whispered. "Then you won't seem

too huge to her."

"We'll never get her!" Melanie whined.

"Of course we'll get her. Chickens are not very smart. Throw her some more feed."

Slowly, her neck stretched forward, the hen came closer. She still kept shooting concerned looks at the other girls. Freya had to suppress a giggle. Finally, Kokoschka stood right in front of Charlie. She quickly pecked up some of the feed around Charlie's feet. That's when Charlie grabbed her. Kokoschka cackled in protest. She kicked her red legs and jerked her neck left and right, but Charlie held on tight.

"One down," she said, throwing Kokoschka over the fence into the pen where the hen retreated into a quiet corner under offended clucks. "But where are the others?" Charlie looked around desperately. The other girls had never seen her so upset.

"No worries, we'll find them!" Freya tried to console her. "They can't have gotten far."

"You don't understand!" Charlie cried out. Her lip was trembling again. "My gran's going to kill me if even one of her hens goes missing."

"Come, come. Calm down!" Melanie said, patting Charlie's arm. "Nobody is going to kill anybody over a silly hen."

Charlie pushed Melanie's hand away.

"Maybe not, but I'll never be allowed to come here again," she barked. "Come on, let's keep looking."

Downhearted, the others followed her.

They found Huberta and Dolly in the salad patch of the neighbor to the left, and Emma and Clara in the high grass on the other side of the road. The neighbor screeched like a magpie about her tattered lettuces, and Emma got them into trouble with a driver on whose windscreen she had landed. Only Isolde was nowhere to be seen.

Scratched, sweaty, and tired, the *Wild Chicks* finally gave up the search and returned to Grandma Stalberg's kitchen. The bunch of keys and the note were still lying on the middle of the table, but right now nobody was particularly interested in mysteries.

"Just wait 'til I get hold of them," Charlie muttered darkly.

Melanie looked at the kitchen clock. "Oh no, I have to get home. But first I have to catch my breath."

"I don't get it," Trudie whined. "How did they know we were meeting here today?"

"Maybe we have a traitor in our midst." Charlie let her eyes wander over the other three girls' sweaty faces. Her glance fell on Melanie.

Melanie returned her look angrily. "What are you looking at me for? Maybe you blabbered about it."

The two of them stared at each other across the table.

"I'm not the one who hangs around with the boys all the time!" Charlie growled.

"We can't all be such boy-haters like you," Melanie hissed back.

"Please, stop!" Trudie cried out. She was close to tears.

"Yes, that's enough!" Freya slammed her fist on the table. "That traitor-stuff is nonsense. The boys all know where Charlie's gran lives. They just had to follow one of us here. You know exactly how much they love doing that sort of stuff. And Fred's probably smart enough to have noticed that the four of us are having our meetings on the toilets again." She shot Charlie an angry look. "It really isn't such a super-secret meeting place."

Embarrassed, Charlie looked down at her scratched hands. "Sorry, Melanie. I'm…I'm just a bit upset because Isolde is gone."

Melanie shrugged as she got up. "Forget about it. I am so beat! Shall we meet tomorrow?"

"If you'd like," Charlie muttered ruefully. She was still staring at her hands.

"Of course! We still have to solve the mystery of the black key," Melanie chirped. "But now I really have to go."

CHAPTER 5

Charlie found everything she needed in the garden shed—twine, a small hand-cranked drill, an old flower-box, and lots of empty tins. Gran Stalberg always held on to all her empty tins and jars. She used them to collect nails, buttons, and lots of other knick-knacks. Charlie also spotted three mousetraps which her grandma had freshly loaded with bacon before her departure. Charlie let them all snap shut. Then she dragged the tins and everything to the garden gate. There was still no sign of Isolde anywhere.

"Just you wait," Charlie muttered while she grabbed the hand-drill to make some holes in the sides of the tins. She tried not to think of all the terrible things that might have happened to Isolde, but that didn't work very well at all. She was sick with worry, and from being afraid of what her gran might say.

She placed the flower-box upside-down behind the hedge, so that it could not be seen from the gate. Next, she threaded the twine through the holes in the tins and lined them all up on the flower-box. Then she tied the long end of the twine to the latch of the gate. She inspected her contraption, her face set in a fierce expression. *Yes, this would work.* As soon as someone tried to open the gate the tins would fall off the flower-box, making a noise that she could hear from inside the house. Charlie gave it a try, just to be on the safe side. The result was impressive. Gran's permanently grumpy neighbor, Mr. Stoutspeck, peered over the hedge and barked: "What's going on here?", and at least three dogs started barking. Well, if that didn't send any spying *Pygmies* packing, then nothing would.

Charlie carefully put the tins back on the flower-box. Then she ran over to the henhouse. The hens were all already sitting on their perches, their eyes firmly closed and their feathers all fluffed up. They just clucked sleepily when Charlie came in to check for eggs once more. Emma was sitting right by the door, Kokoschka behind her, next to Huberta. Charlie was always amazed by how early chickens went to sleep. Gran Stalberg had once explained to her that it was always the weakest hen that sat right by the door. The strongest always sat in the middle. That was the warmest spot during cool nights. On cold winter nights, each hen might even tuck her comb under the backside of the one in front so that it wouldn't freeze.

Usually it was Isolde who sat in the middle.

If Fred or any one of those stupid Pygmies were here right now, Charlie thought, *I would kick his butt so hard he wouldn't be able sit down for days.*

There were three eggs in the nests, which were of course

not real nests, but small wooden boxes that were padded with straw and had a limestone egg in them to make the hens lay more eggs.

Charlie carefully took out the eggs. "Sleep tight!" she said. Then she quietly stepped outside and latched the door behind her. The henhouse had a small outer room where Charlie's gran kept the straw and bags with the feed. Charlie put the eggs on the straw and filled an old flowerpot with feed before running outside again.

It was still warm. Next door someone was mowing the lawn and two cats were fighting noisily somewhere nearby. *Cats! No way*, Charlie thought. Isolde would have no trouble dealing with a cat.

Charlie was just laying a trail of chicken feed from the gate to the henhouse when she heard the phone ring. She ran into the house. "Hello? This is the Stalberg residence," she said breathlessly.

"Where did you just come from?" her gran hissed into her ear. "I heard it ring at least ten times."

"Me? Why? I was in the garden," Charlie stuttered. Her heart was beating so loud that she thought her grandma must be able to hear it.

"Is something wrong?"

"Why? No. Everything is fine." Charlie's gran always knew when Charlie was lying, because she always blushed when she did. "As red as cherry jam," Gran Stalberg would say. But luckily she couldn't see Charlie's face through the phone.

"Hmm. You better be keeping that henhouse latched. You know how easily that door swings open," she said.

"Of course!" *If she knew,* Charlie thought, *she'd tear my head right off!*

"You sound strange," Gran Stalberg barked down the phone. "Are you ill?"

"No!" Charlie replied. "I'm great. Really!"

"All right, then," Grandma Stalberg cleared her throat. "And what are you still doing there anyway? Shouldn't you be home by now?"

"Mum's still working," Charlie muttered.

"What did you say? Stop mumbling like that!"

"Mum—is—still—working!" Charlie repeated.

"Your mother works too much."

"What else is she going to do?" Charlie retorted. She stuck her tongue out at the phone.

"Take care," Grandma Stalberg grunted, then slammed down the phone. That's how she always ended her phone calls—just plonked down the receiver. *If I ever did that…* Charlie thought. Then she grabbed her school bag and sat down at the kitchen table to do her homework. Even though she was all shaky with rage. And sick worrying about Isolde.

Charlie woke up from the tins rattling outside. Startled, she shot up—and realized that she was still sitting at the kitchen table. It was pitch black outside.

Damn! I fell asleep!—she thought. Her heart was beating wildly, right up in her throat. *Who could that be out there?* The *Pygmies* must all be lying in their beds by now. With bated breath, Charlie crept down the dark corridor toward the front door. What if this was a real burglar? Or someone who was looking for Grandma Stalberg's treasure? Charlie carefully opened the door and peered outside.

There wasn't much to be seen in the darkness, of course. But she could hear someone cursing. And that someone was coming toward the house! Charlie's hand closed around the door handle. *Back into the kitchen*, she thought. *To the phone.* But she was stiff from fear.

"Charlie? Goddammit, switch on the light. What's that nonsense with the tins? You want me to break my legs?"

"Mum?" Charlie asked, dumbfounded. "How…? Where did you come from?"

"I nearly fell asleep behind the wheel," Charlie's mum replied. Her tired face appeared out of the darkness. "And so I thought I might go home early and surprise my daughter. And when I get there, what do I find?" She sighed as she leaned against the door frame. "A note: 'Mum, I'm sleeping at gran's.' That's it. You know full well that I would have never allowed it—it's far too lonely out here."

"Sorry!" Charlie mumbled. "I just wasn't in the mood to stay in the empty flat."

"It's alright," her mother pulled her closer. "But please don't do it again, okay? Promise?"

Charlie nodded.

Her mother kissed her on the head and then they went into the kitchen.

"You weren't even sleeping," Charlie's mum observed. "And how are you planning on getting through the school day tomorrow? Hmm?" She rubbed her knee.

"What's wrong?" Charlie asked with concern.

"That's thanks to your alarm system out there. That's what that was supposed to be, right? Jeez, I nearly died from shock!"

"That was meant for the *Pygmies*." Charlie gathered up her school things. "Shall I make you a tea?"

"Yes, please!" Her mother yawned. "What pygmies?"

"Oh, that's Fred's gang," Charlie explained. "I had a meeting here with my gang today, and the boys spied on us, and then they let the hens out."

"Oh no! Gran's hens?" Charlie's mum dropped wearily on to the kitchen bench and put her feet up on a chair. "I hope they're all accounted for."

"No, they are not!" Charlie sighed. She sniffed at the various tea tins. "It's awful. Isolde is gone!" Charlie's eyes immediately teared up. She quickly wiped them dry with her sleeve. "Do you want rose petal or coconut tea?"

The only luxury Grandma Stalberg indulged in was her

collection of strange teas.

"Rose petal," her mum said. "There'll be trouble when Gran gets back. What are we going to do?"

"Maybe Isolde finds her way back tonight," Charlie replied. "She's much smarter than the other hens." But she didn't sound overly confident. Charlie carefully poured the boiling water over the tea. The whole kitchen immediately smelled of roses.

"You know what?" her mum suddenly said. "We'll have some tea and then we'll go out and find Isolde. I have a flashlight."

"That would be great!" Charlie sniffed. The tears were coming back again. "I really am terribly worried."

It really was a pitch black night. The street on which Grandma Stalberg lived only had a couple of streetlights, and the beam of Charlie's mum's flashlight zigzagged through the darkness like a thin white finger.

"Isolde is the white one, right?" her mum asked quietly.

"Uh-huh." Charlie nodded.

"That should make it easier."

Unless she's been eaten, or run over by a car, Charlie thought.

They swept their flashlight over the wild meadows, underneath the hedgerows, and into the gardens. They stirred up two cats and one fat hedgehog, but there was no sign of a white hen. When they reached the end of the street Charlie's mum stopped. She shook her head as she pointed the beam into the forest that stretched out from there for miles.

"If Isolde went in there we'll never find her," she said. "And, to be honest, I really don't want to go traipsing through the woods at this time of night. I'm sorry."

Charlie looked at her unhappily. "But what are we going to do?" she asked.

"Come on," her mother said. She put her arm around her daughter's shoulders and together they started walking back toward the house. "I promise, we'll think of something."

But Charlie kept looking around.

"We'll talk to your grandma together," her mother said. "And the best thing is to simply tell her the truth—that it wasn't your fault and that the boys wanted to play a prank and—"

"We can't do that!" Charlie shrieked. "That means Gran will find out that I brought the others here. She's forbidden that!" There was no holding back now. Charlie started sobbing.

Confused, her mother squeezed her closer. "She forbade it?" she asked quietly.

Charlie nodded. She awkwardly wiped her sleeve over her face.

Her mother hugged her daughter and stayed silent.

"The boys will pay for this!" Charlie sobbed. "I swear, or I shall drop dead."

"They will have to buy you a new hen," her mother suggested. "And it will have to be as white as Isolde. Maybe Gran won't notice it."

"Hmm." A far too lenient punishment in Charlie's eyes. And anyway, Grandma Stalberg would definitely notice the switch. Charlie was completely drained as she pushed open the gate. They had already cleared away the alarm system.

"Charlie, look!" her mother whispered. "Over there, on the cabbage patch." There was something white between the cabbage heads.

"You better stay here," Charlie whispered excitedly. "I'll handle this." Bent over and very slowly, Charlie approached the white spot in the darkness. "Hey, Isolde?" she whispered. "Hey, my sweet, beautiful Isolde?"

The hen clucked and stretched her neck. But when Charlie knelt in front of her on the cool ground, the hen squatted down and clucked contently.

Very carefully, Charlie pushed a hand underneath the hen's warm belly. Then she placed her other hand on the wings and gently lifted the hen up from the ground.

"Oh, Isolde!" she said, pushing her face into the soft feathers. Then she carried her favorite hen back into the henhouse and put her between the others on the perch.

"Well," her mother said as Charlie came out of the henhouse again, "So now we can go home and relax, right?"

"Right. I'll just lock up quickly." Charlie ran back to the

house. The joy made her skip like a young rabbit. "Oh, mum?" she called as she reached the door. "Do you know what the black key on Gran's key-ring is for?"

"What black key?" her mother yawned.

"Never mind," Charlie said. "Not important."

And then they drove home.

CHAPTER 6

"**A**nd? How was the chicken hunt?" Barry, a.k.a. Baz, screamed at Charlie as she entered the classroom the next morning. Baz was the smallest and the loudest member of the *Pygmies*, and in Charlie's opinion he was absolutely expendable. He was always cracking jokes that only he got.

The other *Pygmies* were also already there: Fred was sitting on the back of his chair, grinning, and happily tugging his big jug-ears. The *Pygmy* earring hung quite visibly from his left earlobe. Next to Fred sat Big Steve, chuckling stupidly. He was fiddling with his grubby deck of cards, as usual. Steve fancied himself as something of a magician, and he was constantly practicing some boring card trick or another. Standing behind Fred and Steve, tall and broad-shouldered, was the fourth gang member: Willie, also generally referred to as the Choker. His preferred method of ending an argument was the headlock. As usual, Willy was presenting his best Frankenstein expression.

Without a word, Charlie walked past the *Pygmies* and sat down on her chair.

"The stuff we already had to listen to!" Freya moaned. "Unbearable. Melanie is the only one they don't poke fun at."

"Of course!" Charlie growled. All the boys adored Melanie. Pretty Melanie. Wonderful Melanie. She was sitting on the windowsill with Trudie, her face all blotchy-red, like it always was when she got angry.

"We can't let them get away with what they did yesterday!" Melanie hissed. She shot icy stares at the grinning boys. Baz blew her a kiss. Red with rage, Melanie threw Freya's eraser at him.

The door opened and Mr. Moldman, the rotund biology teacher, rolled into the classroom.

"Next break—meet in the toilets!" Charlie whispered before they all went to their seats. Fred started his clucking again, and Mr. Moldman immediately started interrogating him about the different species of poultry. After that, the lesson progressed in relative peace.

On the first bell, all the *Wild Chicks* jumped to their feet and immediately made their way to the girls' restroom.

"Hey, they are having another toilet-conference!" Baz shouted after them.

Steve added with his squeaky voice: "Why don't you meet in the boys' for a change?" Even Willie the Choker had to grin about that one.

"No way, too much boy stink in there!" Charlie shouted back. "They'll be choking on their stupid jokes soon enough," she whispered to the others.

"Why? Do you have an idea?" Freya asked, looking over her shoulder.

The *Pygmies* were following them at a safe distance, wagging their backsides and pouting their lips.

"Nothing specific," Charlie answered. "But we'll think of something."

They had reached the girls' toilets. "I think they're following us," Trudie whispered anxiously.

"They won't dare to come in here," said Charlie.

And indeed, the *Pygmies* clucked, crowed, and flapped their wings, but they stayed outside.

"Freya, you climb on the lid and keep a lookout," Charlie ordered as they all crammed into the tiny cubicle.

"I thought they wouldn't dare to come in here?" Melanie said.

Charlie shrugged. "You never know with that bunch of idiots."

"Did you find your hen?" Trudie asked.

Charlie nodded and rubbed her nose. "Yes, luckily. But just think how scared the poor thing must have been. For that the *Pygmies* will have to pay."

"Yes, and for their stupid comments, too!" Melanie chimed in. She rubbed her cheeks—there were still two red blotches on them.

"Well, we do have one advantage," said Charlie. "We know

where the *Pygmies* meet."

Freya nodded. "In the wood behind the scrapyard. Everybody knows that."

"Exactly. That's where they built their little shack from all sorts of rubbish."

"No! They have a treehouse now," Melanie interjected. "It's great. All the way up in a dead tree."

"Really?" Charlie eyed her suspiciously. "And how would you know about that?"

Melanie's face turned bright red, all the way up to her blonde curls. "What do you think?" she retorted pertly. "I've been there. Fred invited me."

Charlie whistled admiringly. "Oooh, invited!"

"You're an idiot!" Melanie hissed. "The boys really aren't as bad as you think."

"Really? And what was that yesterday, then?" Charlie hissed back. "Was that also 'not so bad'?"

"Shhh!" Freya suddenly whispered from above. "Baz is here."

"What?" Charlie squeezed past Melanie and the completely dumbfounded Trudie and tore open the cubicle door.

There was Baz. Giggling and wiggling his hips. He had two tiny pigtails on his head.

"Helloohoo?" he warbled through pouted lips. "Heve we already fienished with our seecret meeeting? What a peety!"

Two smaller girls, who had just come in, giggled madly. However, one of the older ones, who was fixing her green hair in front of the mirror, grabbed Baz by the collar and pushed him through the door without a word.

"Thank you!" Freya called down from her lookout perch.

"Don't mention it." The green-haired girl replied. Then she turned her attention to her hair again.

Charlie, Melanie, and Trudie squeezed back into the cubicle.

"So they have a treehouse," Charlie said. "That makes things much easier, of course."

Trudie looked at her in surprise. "How? I don't understand."

"Just think for a second!" Charlie said.

"I know!" Freya blurted out. She jumped down from the toilet seat.

"Of course!" Melanie laughed out loud.

Only Trudie shrugged, still completely lost.

"Okay," Charlie sighed, "I'll explain it to you. Listen…"

CHAPTER 7

After school, Charlie went home with Freya. Freya's mum had invited Charlie over for lunch, and Charlie was quite happy about that. In the past days she'd had to cook for herself—eggs and boiled potatoes. That was the only thing she knew how to cook.

"Just don't start fighting with my brother again," Freya pleaded as they climbed up the stairs to the fourth floor.

"Can't promise you that. He's just such a pain sometimes."

"He's really not that bad. You just don't like boys."

"Exactly. They are all idiots."

Freya sighed. "You're already just as bitchy as your gran. Is that contagious or something?"

That stung. For the next two steps, Charlie silently chewed her lip. If anyone else had said that to her, she would have immediately turned around and gone home. But Freya was one of her best friends. And Freya could really get quite insulted if you left her standing. Once she had not spoken a word to Charlie for a week. A whole week!

That's why Charlie just mumbled: "You're always protecting your brother."

"Not true," said Freya. "But he is my brother. You can't understand it, because you don't have one."

"Thank god for that!" Charlie replied. "That would really be all I need!" *Who would ever wish for a brother?* Definitely not her.

At first, lunch was a peaceful affair. They had spaghetti, especially for Charlie, and Freya's dad told one joke after another until Charlie nearly choked on her food with laughter. Titus, Freya's brother, was luckily quite busy with his spaghetti, which kept him quiet.

But then, just as Charlie was savoring the delicious desert, Freya's mother said: "Freya, I'm meeting the girls for a coffee this afternoon. I'll be back by six. Maybe Charlie would like to keep you company and the two of you can look after Luke? Okay?"

Freya's spoon stopped in mid-air. Charlie forgot to swallow.

"But we're doing something very important this afternoon!" Freya said.

"What's that?" her father asked. "Something for school?"

Charlie and Freya shook their heads.

"Well, then you can probably postpone it until tomorrow, right?"

"Can't Titus look after him for a change?"

"I have football!" Titus interjected through a mouthful of food.

"Freya, really!" her mother said.

Freya stared in silence at her plate.

Charlie kicked her under the table, but Freya still didn't say anything.

Titus happily kept chomping away, as if the whole thing had nothing to do with him. Charlie could have exploded with rage. She gave Freya's mum a pleading look.

"This really is quite important," she said. "Freya has to be there. She really has to."

Freya's mum gave an awkward laugh. "And what is it that's so important? Go on, spit it out, Freya."

Freya shook her head. "I can't. It's secret."

"Ha! Will you listen to that!" Titus chuckled and shook his head.

"That's enough," said Freya's father. "Let's eat in peace. We can't please our children all the time."

"Titus is a boy and that's the only reason he doesn't have to look after Luke," Charlie muttered under her breath. "Just because he's a stupid boy."

Freya's parents looked at her in surprise. Freya still wasn't saying anything. Only her face had turned white.

"But that—is nonsense, Charlotte," Freya's mother said.

"And it's none of your business anyway," Titus growled across the table.

"You just shut up, you brainless sports jock!" Charlie hissed.

"Stop it!" Freya's father interjected angrily. "Next time it'll be Titus' turn to look after Luke, but today it's Freya's job. And now I don't want to hear another word!"

"Agreed?" Freya's mother took her daughter's hand.

Freya looked at her mum—and nodded.

Titus gave Charlie a broad grin. Then he took another helping of spaghetti.

That was too much. Without another word, Charlie got up, ran into the hall, grabbed her bag, and opened the front door. "Just because he's a stupid boy!" she shouted. Then she slammed the door behind her.

The *Wild Chicks* had agreed to meet at the scrapyard. When Charlie arrived all out of breath, Melanie and Trudie were already waiting. Trudie was just devouring one of her favorite chocolate bars.

"Where is Freya?" Melanie asked surprised. "Didn't you two want to come together?"

"Freya has to babysit." Charlie growled.

"Well, I'm glad I don't have a little brother," Melanie sighed.

"Oh, I would love to," Trudie said. "But my parents don't want one."

"We better leave our bikes here," Charlie said. She nudged Melanie. "You go ahead. You know the way."

The small wood where the *Pygmies* had their lair started right behind the fence that surrounded the scrapyard. There were a few footpaths, but the *Wild Chicks* did not use those, of course. For once Melanie was not wearing a dress, but a pair of trousers with tiger stripes, and she led them through the undergrowth and deeper into the wood without hesitation. Soon the scrapyard had disappeared behind them and they were surrounded by nothing but tall trees and ferns.

"It's over there," Melanie whispered. In front of them was a brackish pond, covered with green algae. On its shore stood a tall, old tree. The trunk grew out of the water, and its crown was bare, and in it the *Pygmies* had built their treehouse. It was built from old planks of wood that had been painted in every color imaginable. For a roof the boys had simply used an old sunshade. The floor was covered with carpets from the scrapyard. Leading up to the 'house' was a homemade, rickety ladder.

"Holy cow!" Charlie whispered.

The *Pygmies* were at home. They were sitting on the edge of the platform, their legs dangling over the edge, and they were eating chips.

A radio was blaring all the way down to where the *Wild Chicks* were hiding. "Handy!" Melanie whispered. "With that racket they wouldn't even hear us if we rode up here on an elephant."

"Right!" Trudie chuckled.

"Yes, but they can still see us," Charlie whispered back.

"Absolutely. You get a great view from up there," Melanie

breathed.

"You would know about that, wouldn't you?" Charlie hissed. Melanie made a face at her.

Charlie rubbed her nose. That usually helped her think. But there really wasn't much to think about here.

"We'll just have to risk it," she whispered. "Those shrubs grow nearly all the way to the ladder. And then it's just a matter of speed. Ready?" The other two nodded. "Let's go then!" Charlie whispered. They silently crept toward the treehouse, though that was quite a wasted effort, with all the noise from the radio.

The feet of the *Pygmies* were still dangling happily above their heads.

"This is for Isolde!" Charlie whispered.

And then they ran from under the bushes, over the slippery ground toward the ladder—and pushed it over. As if in slow motion, the ladder swayed through the air, until it finally tilted over and dropped with a loud splash into the pond.

It was all over by the time the stunned faces of Baz, Fred, Steve, and Willie appeared over the edge of the platform.

The *Wild Chicks* performed a victory dance.

"Whoohoooo!" they screamed. "Yieeee-haa!" Green pond scum ran down their arms. The ladder had splattered them all over.

"Heeeey!" Fred screamed. Willie finally switched off the

radio.

"Are you crazy?" Baz's voice nearly cracked. "Put that ladder back!"

But that just triggered another attack of laughter from the *Wild Chicks*.

"Let this be a lesson to you cowards!" Charlie shouted up at them, while Melanie and Trudie were still doubled up with laughter. "Next time you want to pick a fight, come straight to us and don't take it out on some innocent chickens."

"But that was just a joke!" Steve shouted back in his falsetto voice.

"Well, this is also just a joke!" Charlie replied. "Take care, and enjoy the view!"

"What do you mean?!" Fred screamed. In his rage he nearly fell off the tree. "You can't just leave us here."

"Of course we can!" Melanie shouted back. "Yesterday you also just left us to catch the hens."

"You put that ladder back right now!" Will howled. "Or there will be consequences." His face was dark red.

"What consequences?" Charlie asked. "Are you going to send me some air mail, or what?"

Trudie nearly choked on her own laughter.

"Come on!" Charlie took Melanie's and Trudie's arms. "We're off. Oh…" she turned around once more, "I really don't understand how you can be so dim-witted as to not fasten your ladder to the tree."

"Stay here!" Baz screamed.

"Come back!" Fred pleaded.

"We'll get you for this!" Steve howled.

But the *Wild Chicks* had already vanished back into the undergrowth.

CHAPTER 8

An hour later, Charlie, Melanie, and Trudie were sitting next to each other on Grandma Stalberg's couch, still giggling. "Heeey, come baahaaack!" Charlie aped Fred—and the others nearly slid under the table with laughter.

"Baz was twitching around like a mad chimp!" Melanie snorted.

"Please! Stop!" Trudie groaned, wiping tears of laughter from her eyes. "I'm already aching all over."

"Did you see the Choker?" Charlie rolled her eyes just like Willie did when he was angry. "He's becoming serious competition for Frankenstein."

"Sto-hop!" Trudie panted. "Stop it, or I'll explode."

Charlie jumped to her feet. "You know what? We earned ourselves a reward." She fetched Grandma Stalberg's forbidden biscuits from the cupboard and put the large tin on the table. And so what if Gran told her off and then didn't speak to her for three days. It didn't matter. Today none of that mattered.

Delighted, Trudie took a chocolate cookie.

Melanie lifted her biscuit like a champagne glass. "To the greatest gang in the world!" she called. "Cheers!"

Giggling, all three of them stuffed themselves with the forbidden delicacies.

"To the *Wild Chicks*!" Trudie exclaimed—and reached for the next biscuit.

"You know what?" Melanie said. "Now we solve the mystery of the black key."

"Exactly!" Charlie took the key ring from her pocket. Melanie and Trudie eyed the black key with expert expressions.

"Well, it wouldn't fit into a strongbox or something like that!" Melanie declared. "It's too big for that. Looks more like a cellar key."

"My gran doesn't have a cellar," Charlie said. "There's only the larder and the attic."

"Attic sounds good," said Melanie. "Most people hide their secrets in the attic. That's at least how it is in the movies."

Charlie rubbed her nose. "My gran says her attic is haunted."

"Nonsense!" Melanie got up. "She only says that to stop you from snooping around up there."

Charlie mumbled: "Probably." But she still wasn't sure.

Grinning, Melanie pulled Trudie up from the couch. "Definitely. Or do you believe in ghosts? Your gran's quite crafty."

And so Charlie led Melanie and Trudie up the stairs to the second floor, where her gran's bedroom was, as well as the tiny chamber where Charlie slept sometimes.

"Is that your mum?" Melanie stopped in front of one of the many yellowing photographs that hung in tarnished silver frames all over the walls.

Charlie nodded. "That's when she was eighteen, or so."

"And that one, up there?" Trudie stood on her toes. "Is that her as a child?"

"Hmm." Charlie opened the hatch above their heads and pulled down the ladder. She looked suspiciously up at the black hole in the ceiling. Melanie and Trudie were still standing in front of the photos. "You don't really look like your mother at all," Melanie observed. "Did you get your red hair from your dad?"

"No idea," Charlie muttered. "Are you coming or what?"

"Oh, you don't really know your father," Melanie said. She pushed past Charlie and climbed up the ladder. Charlie pressed her lips together. First the thing with the ghosts and now that. Her high spirits were gone.

"You don't even know what he looks like?" Trudie asked inquisitively.

"No! And I don't care, either," Charlie replied testily. "Could we now change the subject, please?" She quickly climbed after Melanie. She'd much rather deal with ghosts that might not exist than with all those questions.

"No father," Trudie mumbled behind her. "Wouldn't that be great?"

Charlie looked around in surprise. Sheepishly, Trudie returned her glance.

"Hey, this is a great attic!" Melanie shouted from above. "Where are you guys?"

"Coming!" Charlie called back. She quickly scaled the last few rungs of the ladder.

"And? Isn't this great?" Melanie said. "Just look at all the stuff up here."

"Great!" said Trudie.

Charlie said nothing. She looked around uneasily. But there was no sign of ghosts or anything like that. "Yep, my gran likes to keep everything," she finally said. "It's annoying, but sometimes it's a good thing."

"I think attics are terribly exciting!" With gleaming eyes, Melanie started rummaging through Grandma Stalberg's boxes and crates. Trudie followed her example. Charlie just stood by the hatch and felt uncomfortable. She tried desperately to feel what she had felt back in the kitchen. But it didn't work. Forbidden biscuits were one thing, but this was different. What if her gran realized that she had been up here? She knew exactly that Charlie would never dare to come up here by herself. She watched uneasily as Trudie and Melanie touched, opened, lifted everything.

"Hey, aren't we looking for a lock or something?" she said, waving the black key at them.

"Yes, yes." Melanie was staring with delight into a huge

chest. "Ooh! Look at this, lots of old dresses. With lace and stuff." She giggled as she put on a tiny hat. "What do I look like?"

"There's a mirror over there," Charlie mumbled. "Have a look yourself."

"What's the matter?" Melanie asked. "What made you go all bitchy?"

"Over here!" Trudie called out excitedly. "There's a lock on this wardrobe. Looks just right."

Melanie and Charlie picked their way toward her.

"How exciting!" Melanie whispered.

Charlie put the black key in the lock. It did go in, but it wouldn't turn. "Doesn't fit," Charlie said disappointedly.

"Doesn't matter!" Melanie said. She looked around. "There's plenty more up here. Look over there, in the corner. That chest that has the shoes on it."

"It's got three locks!" Trudie observed. She sneezed. The dust they had stirred up tickled terribly in their noses.

The three girls climbed over old toys and rolled-up carpets, and then they stood in front of the chest. It had huge drawers, each one secured with a lock.

"Go on, Charlie!" Melanie was all twitchy with excitement. Trudie was intently chewing her thumb-nail.

Charlie put the black key into the topmost lock. She shook her head.

"Doesn't fit either, but…" Charlie pulled the drawer open,

"It's open anyway."

The three *Wild Chicks* peered into the drawer.

In it, neatly folded, were romper suits, bibs, tiny shirts, and baby shoes.

"Oh, Charlie!" Melanie chuckled. "Those must be yours!"

"How cute!" Trudie breathed with delight.

Charlie blushed. "Next one!" she said, quickly pushing the drawer shut. She put the key into the second lock. "Negative!"

But the second drawer was also unlocked, and it contained Charlie's child-clothes—now a number of sizes larger. Lots of hand-knitted jumpers and socks, scarves and gloves, and sprinkled among them, lots of mothballs.

"My gran's also constantly knitting things for me," said Trudie. "They're terribly scratchy."

"My gran's things don't scratch." Charlie sighed as she pushed the drawer shut. "But they are always too small. Or the sleeves are far too long. I always look like a sausage in them. But there's hell to pay if I dare to not wear them. You should hear my gran going on about how ungrateful I am. 'Just like your mother' and so on. I just take something else along for school and quickly get changed on the restroom before first period."

"Your mum and your gran don't get along?" Melanie asked.

Charlie shrugged. "They don't really fight, but they're also never really nice to each other."

The key didn't fit in the third lock either. Charlie wasn't in the mood anymore, anyway, to look into the third drawer.

"My grans are lovely," said Trudie. "Especially one of them. She really belongs in heaven—that's what my father always says."

"My mum and my gran," Melanie pulled some cobwebs from her hair, "Are always fighting. It's actually quite scary. And my gran actually lives with us. I can tell you…"

Trudie pulled the third drawer open and looked inside. "Look! Loads of romantic novels. My grans read that stuff as well."

Surprised, Charlie looked at the piles of thin paperbacks. They had wonderful titles, like *My Heart Beats Only for Doctor Sturgis* or *Love 'til the End*.

"I didn't know my gran reads such things," Charlie mumbled. She leafed through one of the books. Suddenly she had to giggle. "It would be great to tease her with this!"

"Yes, but then she'd know that you've been snooping around up here," said Melanie.

"You're right." Charlie sighed. She suddenly felt uneasy again. But she didn't show it, and the three of them continued their search a little longer.

They found crates full of old porcelain, boxes full of books, and lots of mended clothes. They found a broken sewing machine, a dusty butterfly collection, moldy albums full of stamps, and a box with a wig. But there was no sign of a lock into which the black key might fit. Finally Trudie looked at her watch. "Oh no, it's after six already. I have to get home."

"After six?" Melanie called out in surprise. "I was supposed to go to the shops!"

"We can always carry on tomorrow," said Charlie. "I don't think we'll find anything up here anyway." She no longer wanted to go through Grandma Stalberg's old things, but she didn't say that, of course.

They quickly climbed down the ladder.

"What were you supposed to buy at the shops?"

"Eggs, potatoes, and stuff. Why?"

"No problem!" Charlie latched the ladder. "I have all that here."

Baffled, Melanie looked at her. "Of course! I never thought of that."

Charlie gave an embarrassed laugh. "I'll just quickly lock up the house and then we'll grab some things for you. I'm going home as well. My mum's coming home early today."

When they stepped outside, the sky had clouded over, but the air was still mild and the evening tasted of summer.

Melanie ran over to her bike and brought her shopping bag.

"Here it says…" she frowned at her shopping list. "Ten eggs, two pounds of potatoes, beans, summer savory."

Charlie nodded. "Not a problem." She took the bag from

Melanie and ran off to the vegetable patch. "Let's start with the beans," Charlie said. "Did you know they're poisonous if you eat them raw?"

Melanie and Trudie shook their heads.

With quick fingers, Charlie plucked a small heap of long, slender pods from the small bushes. "These here are the best," she said. "Very tender, and not stringy at all."

Melanie just mumbled: "Oh!"

"How much savory do you need?"

Melanie shrugged helplessly.

Charlie plucked two large handfuls of a dark green herb that grew in neat rows among the beans. "Smell this!" she said proudly, holding the bushels under their noses. "My gran always sows the annual variety. It's much stronger."

Trudie and Melanie looked at each other.

"How do you know all this?" Trudie asked.

"Oh, you just kind of pick it up." Charlie rubbed her nose. She got to her feet and went over to the next vegetable bed, which was quite a bit wider than the bean patch.

"I can't give you quite as many potatoes," she said, plunging her hands into the dark earth. "My gran is quite stingy when it comes to her potatoes. But at least they taste much better than the stuff from the shops."

"Oh, this is great!" Melanie said. "My bag's already quite full. I just need some eggs."

"Coming up!" Charlie jumped to her feet and together

they ran to the henhouse. The hens were of course asleep again. Charlie already had a half-full egg carton in the storeroom. She quickly filled it up from the hens' nests.

"My mum's going to love this!" Melanie said as they ran back to their bikes.

Trudie suddenly giggled. "I wonder how the *Pygmies* are doing."

Charlie cast an expert glance at the sky. "Well, as long as it's not raining…"

"You really think they're still up there?" Now Trudie sounded a little concerned.

"No way. They've probably been rescued by someone walking their dog in the wood," Charlie said. "And if not, then we'll know tomorrow, when school starts. Oh, by the way," Charlie grinned, "Tomorrow you can give me a hand mucking out the henhouse."

"Oh yes, please!" Trudie said excitedly.

"Mucking out?" Melanie screwed up her face. "What does one wear for that?"

"Your best dress, of course!" Charlie replied. For the longest moment she and Melanie just looked at each other. Then both of them grinned.

"See you tomorrow!" Charlie swung herself on to her bike.

"See you tomorrow!" Trudie called after her. "And I hope Freya can come tomorrow."

"Hope so!" Charlie called back. And again, Trudie had managed to spoil her mood.

CHAPTER 9

When Charlie came home, she had a visitor waiting for her.

"Your best friend is waiting for you," her mother said.

"Freya?" Charlie asked.

"Of course Freya!" Her mother looked at her in surprise. "Or do you suddenly have another best friend?"

Charlie shook her head and rubbed her nose vigorously.

"Did you have a fight?"

"Not really."

"Ah. I better not ask any more questions, right?" Her mother shook her head. "Shall I make you some sandwiches?"

"Yes, please!" Charlie slowly walked toward her room. She really wanted to be angry with Freya, but she was just relieved—relieved that she had come because, when she was sulking, Freya could sometimes disappear for days. Even at school she wouldn't speak a word to Charlie, though they sat next to each other in class. She really could be quite stubborn.

But what did Freya have to sulk about? Charlie put her hand on the door handle. *If anybody has the right to be sulking, it should be me*, she thought. Her head and her heart really were in quite a muddle.

Freya was sitting on Charlie's bed. Her eyes were red. She looked lost. She gave Charlie a sheepish smile.

"Hello," she said. "How did it go? Did our plan work?"

Charlie nodded. "You really missed something." She sat down by her desk and stared holes into the carpet. "Melanie and Trudie were great."

"Really?" Freya asked quietly. Then the two of them sat in silence for a few terribly long moments. Freya nibbled on her fingernails and Charlie rubbed her nose. Luckily, Charlie's mum came in and brought the sandwiches.

"What do you want to drink?" she asked. "Hot cocoa?"

"Yes, please!" Freya said. She managed a crooked smile.

Charlie just nodded.

Her mother left and the two were again alone with their silence. Charlie took a salami sandwich—and then put it back on the plate.

"What did you tell the others?" Freya asked.

"That you had to babysit. What else?"

Freya nervously poked around in her ear. The chicken feather hung from a leather band around her neck.

"Thanks for trying to help me," she suddenly said in a tiny voice. She still didn't look at Charlie.

"And why didn't you say anything?" Charlie burst out. "I felt like such an idiot. All of them pretending like they had no idea what I was talking about. Did you see your stupid brother grinning at me? And you just sat there as if it had nothing to do with you. But I was right. I was completely right!"

Freya looked at her hands. "I can't do that," she said, so quietly that Charlie nearly didn't hear her.

"Can't do what?" Charlie shook her head angrily.

"When my mum asks me something, I can't say no. And when my dad chimes in, then…" Freya shrugged.

"Hmm." Charlie grabbed the sandwich again. "Your brother…" she muffled through her full mouth, "…is quite perfect at it."

"He is," Freya mumbled. She bit into a cheese sandwich and sniveled.

"Are you crying?" Charlie asked, startled.

"Nah, I'm fine," Freya answered. She blew her nose. Both were quite happy when finally the door opened and Charlie's mum came in.

"Here's your cocoa," she said, putting a steaming pot and two mugs on the table. "I hope there's enough sugar in there this time. Do you need anything else?"

Charlie shook her head.

"I have to go soon anyway," Freya said. When they were alone again, she said to Charlie: "You don't always fight back either."

"What do you mean?" Charlie frowned—but of course she knew exactly what Freya was talking about.

"Well, with your gran. Do you ever say no to her?"

"That's different," Charlie said angrily. "Nobody says no to my gran. Not even my mum. And when she does, my gran won't speak to us for a fortnight, and I can't stay with her until my mum has apologized. Are your parents like that?"

"No, but…"

"No, they are *not* a bit like that. And you should be bloody happy about it." Charlie fell silent. Her heart was beating wildly and her lips were trembling. She quickly grabbed another sandwich and bit into it.

Freya looked at her, confused. "How was I to know it's that bad? You never told me."

"Well, it's that bad," Charlie said. "And I don't want to talk about it anymore. Nothing I can do about it anyway."

"Maybe you could come to us more often when your mum's working," Freya suggested.

"No, thank you. I'd just fight with your brother all the time," Charlie said, though the thought did make her smile. "We also searched the whole attic for the lock for the black key. While we were safe from the *Pygmies*."

"And?"

"Nothing. And I've already tried all the locks in the rooms. It's really getting quite mysterious. Do you know what I think?"

"What?" Freya slurped her cocoa. It made her feel lovely and warm.

"I think Grandma Stalberg wanted to play a trick on me!"

Charlie whispered. "Wouldn't put it past her."

"Then there's no point looking for the lock," Freya observed.

"Oh yes, there is!" Charlie frowned. "We should keep looking. Wouldn't it be great if we really found a treasure? Those stupid *Pygmies* would probably explode with envy."

"Are we doing anything tomorrow?" Freya asked. She added shyly: "I don't have to babysit Luke all week. Mum says it's Titus' turn."

"What? Now you tell me?" Charlie asked. "So the whole fight was totally worth it!" She was suddenly mighty proud of herself. "We're mucking out the henhouse tomorrow. Will you come?"

Freya nodded as she got up. "Do you think the boys are still in their treehouse?"

"Nah, definitely not," Charlie answered. And she was right. The *Pygmies* had been home for half an hour. And they were seething with rage.

CHAPTER 10

Revenge is a strange thing. It never quite seems to find an end.

As Charlie steered her bicycle onto the school yard the next morning, the *Pygmies* jumped her from the bushes. Baz and Steve pulled her from her bike and Willie took her in his signature choke hold.

"Hey, are you crazy?" Charlie panted once she had gotten over the initial shock. "We'll all be late!"

"Just a few minutes, as far as we're concerned," Fred replied with a grin. "You, however, are taking the day off."

They dragged the screaming and kicking Charlie behind the school building. The bell was ringing for first period, and the school yard was completely deserted.

Charlie soon realized that they were headed for the small shed, where Mr. Mouseman, the caretaker, kept his brooms, rakes, and shovels.

"Open it!" Fred said. He still had that smug grin on his face. To Charlie's great surprise, Steve actually produced a key from his pocket.

"Where did you get that?" she asked. "You didn't steal that from Mouseman?"

"No, we just borrowed it!" Steve replied with mock

indignation. "It's his spare key."

"So that's what you're practicing your magic tricks for!" Charlie snorted with disdain. But that moment Willy the Choker already shoved her into the dark shed.

"Oh no!" Melanie's voice came through the windowless darkness. "We were hoping at least you'd get away. That's so embarrassing!"

"They just grabbed us and nobody helped us!" Trudie sounded very upset.

"Well, no point moaning about it." Charlie carefully moved forward, but she stepped on a rake and the stick whacked her in the head. "Ouch! Damn!"

"What is it?" Freya asked with concern.

"Nothing. Does someone have a flashlight?"

"Nope," Melanie answered.

"What a fine gang we are," Charlie moaned. She felt her head. This was going to be one huge bump.

"But they can't just leave us locked up in here!" Trudie sniveled. "School starts soon."

"It already has," Melanie observed. "And it won't be them who'll be in trouble, but us. Or do you think Mrs. Rose is going to believe this story?"

"But she has to!" Trudie whined. "I was already late twice last week. If my dad finds out…"

"Calm down!" said Charlie. "When someone finds us, they can definitely witness that we were locked up in here, right?"

"*If* someone finds us here," Freya added gloomily, "Before we end up as skeletons leaning on the wall."

Trudie groaned.

"Maybe Mouseman comes by here soon," Charlie suggested.

"And maybe he doesn't," Melanie said. "How about we make some noise?"

"Waste of energy," Charlie objected. "There wasn't anyone around when they dragged me here."

"Mrs. Rose doesn't like us being late at all," Freya sighed. "And I'm already on her blacklist. The boys are so mean!"

The others stayed silent.

"After we get out of here…" Charlie growled, "They will wish they were never born."

"How long does it take to starve to death?" Trudie asked.

"You'd die of thirst first!" Freya said.

"Or suffocate," Charlie muttered. "The air in here is horrible."

"You know what?" Melanie said. "The whole revenge thing is really getting on my nerves. Is this just going to go on and on? Next, *we* will think of some revenge and then *them*, and so on. It's really boring!"

"They started it!" Charlie objected.

From outside came the sound of steps—and the melody of *Yankee Doodle*. Mr. Mouseman always whistled that tune.

Immediately, all of the *Wild Chicks* started pounding

against the walls.

"Open up!" they all screamed in unison. "Open up, Mr. Mouseman, please!"

The door opened and they girls squinted into the light. Mr. Mouseman stood in the open door.

"How did you get in here?" he asked baffled.

"We were…" Trudie began.

"It was this huge guy!" Charlie quickly interrupted her. "He just grabbed us and put us in here."

"What? All of you at the same time?" Mr. Mouseman sounded dubious. "That really must have been one big guy!"

"No. One after another, of course," Charlie said.

"He was probably a kidnapper," Melanie added. "They do that sort of thing."

"Hmm. Right. And how did he get my key?" Mr. Mouseman asked.

"How should we know?" Charlie asked tetchily.

"Real gangsters always have lock picks!" Freya explained.

"Real gangsters?" Poor Mr. Mouseman looked even more confused now.

"We have to go to class," Charlie quickly said, pushing past the caretaker.

"Yes, and thanks for freeing us!" Freya said before storming off after Charlie.

"And why shouldn't I say who it really was?" Trudie asked as they all jogged toward the school building.

"Because that's not the way it's done," Charlie answered impatiently.

"I don't get it!" Trudie was gasping for air.

"Melanie, you explain it to her!" Charlie sighed. She suddenly veered off toward the bike stands.

"What are you doing?" Melanie shouted after her. "Mrs. Rose will be way mad already."

Charlie didn't answer. She walked along the rows of bicycles. "Here we are!" she said finally. "All right next to each other. How handy!"

She quickly opened the tire valves on all four bikes. And because she wasn't quite sure whether the next one might not also be a *Pygmy* bike, she let the air out of that one as well.

"Oh Charlie, don't do that!" Freya pleaded.

"This is really stupid!" Melanie declared. "I'm going inside. Come on, Trudie."

The two of them ran toward the entrance.

Freya hesitantly stepped next to Charlie. "Don't you think it's enough?" she asked.

"Done!" Charlie said. She giggled. "Can't wait to see their faces."

Freya shook her head.

"Oh, stop being such a sourpuss! Come on!" Charlie took her by the arm and dragged her along. "Hey! Wait!" she shouted after Melanie and Trudie. They caught up with them on the front steps.

Mrs. Rose listened to the kidnapper story with a deep frown and pursed lips. Meanwhile Fred, Steve, Baz and Willie sat stiff as planks and stared into their books.

"Come on! How daft do you think I am?" Mrs. Rose asked when Charlie finally shut her mouth. "First these four heroes there—who now suddenly seem very intent on reading their textbooks—turn up late, and then you give me this outrageous story."

"But it's true!" Charlie replied meekly.

"Yes, of course. And I still believe in Father Christmas. Sit down!"

The *Wild Chicks* skulked off to their seats. Mrs. Rose picked up her little black book and made four marks.

"The line with my name must look like a graveyard by now!" Charlie hissed into Freya's ear.

"Do you want to know what I think?" Mrs. Rose said as she dropped the book back into her shiny red bag. "I think we are having ourselves a little gang war. And since I believe gangs are probably the silliest thing on this planet, I now advise all of you to never be late again because of these shenanigans. Have I made myself quite clear?"

The *Wild Chicks* nodded.

"And you? Did you get the message as well?"

The *Pygmies* muttered something.

"Fine. Then let's get your brains refocused on your work. Fred? To the blackboard, if you please."

CHAPTER 11

That afternoon, Trudie was the first to arrive at Grandma Stalberg's house. There was no sign yet of the others. She was just opening the garden gate when she heard something rustling in the bushes behind her. She spun around—but there was nothing to be seen. A fat dachshund was trotting across the street, and next door a cat was sunbathing on the rubbish bins.

That's what you get from all that kidnapper talk, Trudie thought angrily. She leaned her bike against the hedge and ran toward the chicken run. The hens twitched their heads curiously when they saw her coming. Then they started crowing miserably, as if they hadn't been fed in days.

Trudie opened the door to the henhouse to fetch some feed, but then she again heard something. She couldn't tell what it was, but it did sound suspicious. And it came from the currant bushes.

"Somebody there?" she asked hesitantly.

"Of course!" Charlie called out behind her, pushing open the garden gate. "Why are you looking so weird?" Freya was with her as well.

"Nothing!" Trudie sighed with relief. A huge blackbird came out of the currant bushes to pick at the gravel path. "I'm seeing ghosts."

"Happens to me all the time," Charlie said. "Especially when I'm alone. I sometimes think my granddad is haunting this place."

At that moment, Melanie arrived.

"I don't believe it!" Charlie exclaimed. "Melanie. In jeans!"

Melanie stuck her tongue out and leaned her bike on the hedge. "We're probably the only gang ever that mucks out henhouses together," she said with a sigh.

"I think it's going to be fun!" said Trudie.

"I'd rather solve the mystery of the black key!" said Freya. "I already missed the last treasure hunt."

"Business before pleasure!" Charlie answered. "Come on!"

"And how long does one smell of chicken poo after this?" Melanie asked as she trudged after the others.

"A week? A month?" Charlie snickered.

"If it's still this hot later, maybe we can all get under the garden hose?" Freya suggested.

"Oh yes!" Trudie cried out.

Two of the hens were hiding from the summer heat inside the henhouse. But when the four girls turned up with their pitchforks, buckets, and shovels, they quickly escaped into the run, cackling their protest.

"First, all this straw has to come out!" Charlie ordered. "Just chuck it through the window onto the dung heap. Then we'll scratch the poo from the perches and put new straw underneath. Oh, and, most importantly, the nests. They have to be cleaned thoroughly, and the lime eggs have to be cleaned too."

"What are the lime eggs for?" Freya asked.

"Gran says hens prefer to lay eggs next to one that's already there, rather than into an empty nest," Charlie explained. "And maybe that way they also think we're not stealing all of their eggs. You have no idea how often I've dragged these stupid lime eggs into the house, thinking they were the real thing."

"I want to do the nests," Trudie called out. "May I?"

"There's poo everywhere!" Melanie moaned. "And this is all from those few scrawny hens?"

Charlie laughed. "Well, nobody has invented a chicken toilet yet. And my gran always says: chicken shit is worth its weight in gold."

"How that?" Melanie's face was screwed up in disgust as she scraped the perches with a small shovel.

"What do you think makes all those veggies grow so well out there? Chicken shit is the best fertilizer ever. You just have to remember to mix it with straw and soil, or else it's too hot."

"Or else it's *what*?" Trudie asked.

"Hot. Too sulphurous. Too strong." Charlie explained. "That would just make the vegetables shoot up too fast, without getting any flavor. Oops! I hope we have enough fresh straw."

"You do know a lot about this stuff!" Freya mumbled as she hauled the straw through the window.

"What do we do with the eggs?" asked Trudie.

"Put them in the front room there," Charlie said.

"Hey, there are some more here!" Freya called out. "All the way back here, underneath the perch."

"Oh, another secret nest!" Charlie said. "They do that sometimes. Maybe we'll find even more."

"Well, it's not fair that they get their eggs stolen all the time," Melanie said. She was intently scraping the ground beneath the perches.

"Would they all turn into little chicks?" Trudie asked. She looked uneasily at the egg in her hand.

"Nonsense!" Charlie giggled. "How would that work without a rooster?"

"Ah…right!" Trudie muttered, her face turned bright red.

"Don't worry!" Charlie said to her. "The hens also think they have chicks in them. Sometimes they even sit on them and try to hatch them."

After an hour, the henhouse was so clean that even Grandma Stalberg wouldn't have found anything to complain about. The fresh hey smelled wonderful, and the girls were altogether quite satisfied with themselves.

"And now let's hose ourselves down!" Charlie suggested. "In the back, by the water barrel. Nobody can see us there."

"Yuck! My clothes are soaked through with sweat," Freya said. "Do you have anything fresh I could wear?"

"I brought something," Melanie said. She ran to her bike and came back with a big plastic bag.

"I don't believe it!" Charlie said, rolling her eyes. She quickly fetched some fresh t-shirts for Freya and Trudie. Grandma Stalberg's rain barrel was behind the house on a small bricked patio. It was surrounded by high lilac bushes. The girls hung their sweaty clothes over the bushes and put the fresh ones on a chair, a safe distance from the hose. And then Charlie turned on the ice cold water.

Screaming and laughing, the girls jumped around in the cold jet of water. They squirted each other and danced on the slippery bricks until their lips were blue from the cold.

It happened just as Charlie ran to turn off the water.

A couple of arms appeared through the lilac and pulled the clothes from the branches. They also grabbed the fresh clothes from the chair, and Melanie's plastic bag. It all happened so quickly that the girls just stood there and watched.

"Hullohoo!" It came from the bushes. Three boys' heads grinned at them.

"Tsk, tsk!" Baz warbled. "That's not very proper. What if the neighbors see you like that?"

"Go away!" Charlie yelled. Freya hid behind the rain barrel, and Melanie and Trudie stood behind Charlie's back.

"We're going!" Baz said. "But we're taking your clothes with us. You'll get them back tomorrow. But you better not come to school like that!"

Steve giggled hysterically. Willie's face just turned dark red and he stared down at his shoes. But then the lilac branches closed together again and the boys were gone—as were the girls' clothes.

"You perverts!" Melanie shouted after them. Shivering, they all ran to the bushes to peer through them. They saw the thieves run off across Grandma Stalberg's vegetable beds, the clothes bundled up in their arms.

"Stop!" Charlie screamed. "You little shits!"

But the boys just waved at them and blew them kisses. Then they disappeared through the gate.

The *Wild Chicks* stood there, shaking with cold, looking at each other. Freya came out from behind the rain barrel.

"That's what I heard earlier," Trudie said. "They were here the whole time. Definitely."

"Where? What are you talking about?" Charlie asked.

"In the currant bushes," Trudie answered. "I heard rustling in there earlier."

"And you didn't tell us?" Charlie screamed at her.

"I thought...I..." Sobbing, Trudie pressed her hands to her wet face.

"Leave her alone!" Melanie hissed at Charlie. "That's where all this stupid gang stuff has gotten us."

"Okay, okay. I didn't mean it," Charlie muttered.

"Come on, let's go inside and find something to wear," Freya said. "Or do you all want to die of pneumonia?"

Huddling together, the stark naked *Wild Chicks* made a dash for the house. Of course, that very moment, Mr. Stoutspeck's head poked over the hedge. "What are you looking at?" Charlie shouted at him before she also vanished through the front door. She didn't even want to think about the things her gran would hear from her dear neighbor on her return.

CHAPTER 12

Luckily Melanie thought of the clothes in the attic. It was great fun putting on the weird things that hung down over their feet and made them all look like shrunken adults. Once they sat, transformed, around the kitchen table, sipping blackberry tea and eating forbidden biscuits, they were nearly ready to find the revenge of the *Pygmies* quite funny. Until Charlie suddenly sat bolt upright and put her mug down on the table with a bang.

"What is it?" Freya asked, startled.

"The key!" Charlie said. "Holy cow, they have the key."

"Are you sure?" Trudie breathed.

"Of course. It was in my trousers!"

They looked at each other in shock.

"When did you hear the rustling in the bushes, Trudie?"

"That was already before you all arrived."

Charlie groaned.

"And I was babbling about a treasure," Freya said in dismay.

"Yes, you did," said Melanie. "And you even mentioned the black key. So, if they didn't hear about it during their last snoop-attack, they definitely know now."

"But that's awful!" Trudie whined. "What are we going to

do?"

"Much more importantly: what are *they* going to do? We have to find out. Pronto." Charlie could no longer sit in her chair. She jumped up with a grim face, but then she looked in shock down at herself. "Damn, I'd forgotten about those stupid clothes. Never mind. Come on!"

"Okay, but where?" Trudie shouted after her.

"To the treehouse, of course," Melanie said. She deftly picked up her long skirt and ran after Charlie.

Freya was not quite so deft. She stepped on the hem of her dress and fell flat on the floor. She struggled back to her feet and ran after the others. Trudie stumbled out of the house last, her dress gathered all the way over her bare knees.

"No way can you ride a bike in these rags!" Freya shouted.

"Well, there isn't going to be any cycling anyway!" Charlie growled. She was standing next to the flat bikes, her face dark red. "But boy are they going to be sorry." With huge steps, Charlie ran back to the house. Melanie, Trudie, and Freya looked after her.

"What's she doing now?" Melanie asked. Trudie and Freya just shrugged and walked back to the house.

Charlie was standing by the phone. "Fine. See you then." She had a malicious smile on her face as she put down the receiver. "My mum's picking us up in her taxi in ten minutes. She'll take us to the scrapyard."

"You want to creep around the forest…" Freya plucked

at the lace and frills dangling around her legs, "…in these things?"

"Do you have a better idea?" Charlie asked angrily. "Do you think I'm just going to sit here calmly and wait until they turn up with the key and steal Gran's treasure?"

Trudie opened her mouth to say something, but that moment the phone rang. Charlie picked it up and turned as white as cottage cheese.

"Oh, hi, Gran…no, I just thought it might be Mum. Yes, of course, everything's fine."

Melanie suppressed a laugh. Freya screwed her face. Charlie still looked quite pale.

"Just today we—ehm—I cleaned up here. The weeds? Well…they're growing." Freya rolled her eyes. "Of course, definitely."

A car honked outside. Melanie ran to the window and peered out.

"Your mum!" she whispered.

"Gran? I have to go. Mum's picking us up right now. What? Did I say *us*? No, just a slip of the tongue. Of course I'm alone. I know. No strangers. No. Yes. Yes. Bye, then. Yes, bye."

Charlie heaved a deep sigh as she put down the phone. To her great surprise, she realized that her heart wasn't beating half as fast as it usually did after her gran's calls. And that even though she had lied to her.

"You know what?" Charlie said to the other *Wild Chicks*. "You should always stand next to me when my gran calls. Makes it less horrible, somehow."

They stepped outside and Charlie locked the door.

"Did I say *us*?" Melanie said in a squeaky voice. "No, just a slip of the tongue."

Giggling, they ran toward the gate.

"Doesn't she allow you to have anyone over?" Trudie asked.

"On pain of death!" said Charlie. "My gran usually assumes the worst from other people. Trust no one—that's her motto."

"Not even your friends?" Melanie asked. Charlie's mum was already waving at them.

Charlie waved back and opened the gate. "There's no such thing as friends as far as my gran is concerned. She thinks everyone wants to cheat her, or rob her, or steal her handbag."

"Oh dear," Freya mumbled.

"And?" Charlie's mother called toward them. "May your driver inquire what you are planning and what is up with that strange attire?"

"Sorry, Mum," said Charlie. She dropped into the passenger seat. "But what we're planning is top secret."

CHAPTER 13

"**I** only see three pairs of feet!" Freya whispered. They had already snuck quite close to the treehouse of the *Pygmies*, and the owners' dirty feet were dangling quite visibly above their heads. The boys had tied string to some crooked branches and let them hang into the pond's green water. They were probably supposed to be some kind of fishing rods.

"Maybe they posted a lookout!" Trudie whispered. She cast a worried glance around them.

"Wait here. I'll do a quick recon," Melanie hissed. Despite the long dress, she vanished as nimbly as a cat into the undergrowth. An empty drink can flew down from the treehouse into the water.

"Hey, Baz. Stop that!" Fred shouted. "You want it to look like the scrapyard around here, or what?"

"Okay, okay!" Baz replied.

"And enough with the partying anyway. It's time to make a plan!" Fred said.

"Oh yes!" Willie's chimed in. "Do you have an idea, boss?"

"Boss!" Freya giggled.

"Looks like we came at the right time," Charlie muttered.

The bushes behind them rustled and Melanie sat down

in the grass next to them. "Steve's sitting in the bushes about twenty yards from here," she whispered. "But he's totally absorbed in some card trick."

That very moment Fred shouted from above: "Hey, Steve? Are you keeping watch?"

"Ye-es!" Steve's shrill voice came from the undergrowth.

"Fine," Fred said. "Then I'll tell you my plan."

"I hope it's not one of those complicated ones," Willie groaned.

"No. Even you should be able to understand it," Fred replied. "First, we have to make sure that those stupid chicks are home tonight."

"Why shouldn't they be at home?" Willie sounded puzzled.

"Jeez, you are dense sometimes," Fred sighed. "Because they know we have the key."

"No way!" Baz sneered. "I bet they're all going to cry in mama's lap tonight. *If* they manage to get home without clothes."

The *Pygmies'* legs kicked with laughter. The *Wild Chicks* were boiling with rage.

"Seriously now!" Fred said in his commander voice. "I'll find out whether Charlie's at home."

"You better hope her mum's home," Baz said. "Otherwise she'll be sleeping at her gran's."

"How would you know that?" Willie asked with awe.

"I know stuff," Baz said. "I have my sources."

"Okay, let's hope for the best," Fred continued. "You take care of the rest. Baz checks up on Trudie, Willie Melanie, and Steve Freya. Did you get that, Steve?"

"Yes yes!" Steve shouted back.

"Oh man, Willie!" Baz groaned, clicking his tongue. "You're lucky. Pretty Melanie! Whoohooo! I just got old Trudie!"

Willie giggled awkwardly.

"Those little shits!" Melanie hissed. Trudie chewed her lip self-consciously.

"But how are we going to find out whether they're at home?" Willie asked.

"The phone, maybe, you dimwit?"

Baz warbled: "Hulloho? Thees eez Elisabeeth. Is my deeer friend Melanie at home?"

"Exactly!" said Fred. "And then you immediately notify me. Got it? And if Charlie doesn't muck things up, we meet at my place at nine. My parents are going to be out tonight. Opera or something."

"Lucky you!" Steve shouted from below. "And what am I supposed to tell my parents?"

"Just tell them that you're sleeping over at my place," Fred suggested.

"My parents will never let me do that," Willie said. "I'll have to sneak out. But I have to be home by eleven—that's when my dad gets back from work. And if he catches me, there'll be hell to pay."

"Is he still being a shit to you?" Fred asked him, so quietly that the *Wild Chicks* could barely hear him.

"Don't want to talk about it," Willie grumbled.

The treehouse fell silent for a moment.

Then Baz shouted: "Hey, I think something's biting!" He quickly pulled up the string, but there was nothing on it except for some dripping pond scum.

"Jeez, how often do I have to tell you not to yank it out like that?" Willie groaned.

"This fishing stuff is stupid anyway," said Fred. "Stupid and boring."

"You're just saying that because you're the only one who hasn't caught anything," Baz taunted him. "So, we meet at nine at your place. Then we go to the grandma's house. And then what?"

"And then, and then," Fred said angrily. "You'll see what then. The girls haven't found that treasure yet either. So it won't be easy."

"But I'm not going into the chicken house!" Baz declared. "Just so we're clear!"

"Me neither," said Willie. "My granddad told me where there's chickens, there's rats."

The *Wild Chicks* grinned at each other.

"Very funny!" Fred hissed at them. "Did you forget our pledge?"

"No, why?"

"We pledge," Fred said with a somber voice, "To protect life, honor, and justice, without fear, against criminals, pirates, Nazis, cannibals, and nasty teachers."

"See?" said Baz. "Not a word about chickens."

Suddenly Steve appeared next to the ladder. "I got it!" he shouted up. "A super trick! Wait 'till you see this." He panted up the crooked ladder.

"Hey, you're supposed to keep watch!" Fred barked at him. "Not playing with you stupid cards."

"Sod that!" Steve chuckled as he hoisted himself on to the platform. A moment later, his feet joined the others above the pond.

"What am I keeping watch for? You seriously think the girls will come here, naked, and on foot? Or what?"

Even Fred had to laugh about that.

"Just you wait. You won't be laughing long!" Charlie hissed, angrily rubbing her nose.

"Right, now check out the best trick you'll ever see," Steve said excitedly. "Here it comes…"

"We don't want to see your stupid trick!" Fred barked. "Jeez, you lot really are lucky the girls can't hear you. These two heroes are afraid of chickens and you can't think of anything but your stupid magic tricks. I can't take it anymore."

"Oh shut up!" Baz retorted angrily. "And who stole the girls' clothes? That was us. You're just always sitting here, mouthing off."

"Then go and find yourself another boss!" Fred roared, jumping to his feet. "Or maybe I should find myself another gang!"

"What a bunch of idiots!" Melanie whispered.

Willie suddenly snorted with laughter. "Jeez, Fred, you really should have seen their faces when we took their clothes. Just like in the movies!"

The *Wild Chicks* had to really restrain themselves not to storm out of their hiding place and throw the *Pygmies* into the scummy sludge of the pond. Above their heads, Steve and Baz were nearly falling off the platform with laughter.

"Don't get too smug with yourselves!" Fred said grumpily. "Those girls are more stupid than chicken shit."

"Just like all girls," Steve agreed.

Trudie and Freya turned as red as toadstools. Charlie clenched her fist. Red blotches appeared on Melanie's face, and she started chewing her blonde locks.

"Exactly," said Baz. "They are all stupid."

"You just shut it!" Fred sneered. He crouched down at the top of the ladder. "And who kept making goo-goo eyes at Melanie? You even wrote her love letters. Saw them with my own eyes!"

"Really?" Steve asked. "And what did she answer?"

Willie was snorting again.

"I just wrote those for a laugh!" Baz said, angrily chucking an empty chips bag into the water.

"I told you to stop that!" Fred said angrily.

"Did he really write you love letters?" Trudie whispered into Melanie's ear.

Melanie nodded. There were too many blotches on her face to count.

"Come on!" Charlie whispered. "We heard enough. My mum's going to be back at the scrapyard in ten minutes."

"One thing I don't get," they heard Willie ask above. "That treasure. If we find it, doesn't it belong to the grandma?"

"Bull!" Fred answered. "A treasure belongs to whoever finds it. That's obvious. It's usually stolen stuff anyway."

"Yeah?" Willie mumbled.

The *Wild Chicks* snuck away as quietly as they had come, their faces set with determination.

CHAPTER 14

Luckily, Charlie's mum had to drive her taxi that night.

"I'm sorry," she said to Charlie. "But there's that big conference, you know. Tonight I can make as much money in one evening as I usually do in a week. And I will be home tomorrow, lunchtime. Okay?"

"No problem, Mum!" Charlie said. "Freya asked me to sleep over anyway."

She really didn't like to lie to her mum, but this time there was no alternative. Charlie of course didn't really trust the *Pygmies* to find Grandma Stalberg's treasure—they were far too brainless for that. But the thought of the boys snooping around Gran's house—trampling all over the carpets with their pond-scummy-shoes, ferreting around in the drawers with their filthy fingers—made her quite sick. No, they had to be stopped, even if that meant having to lie for a change. The thought calmed her conscience. Of course the other *Wild Chicks* didn't tell their parents either that they were staying in Charlie's gran's house alone.

"Can I sleep over at Charlie's?" They asked. "Charlie's mum said it's okay, and we only have third period tomorrow."

"Well, if Charlie's mum allows it," said Freya's father, Trudie's mother, and Melanie's father—which gave all three of them guilty consciences, but was also a great relief. The boys' check-up calls came just after seven. The parents called their daughters to the phones, but when they answered there was suddenly nobody on the other end of the line. Now the *Wild Chicks* knew that the *Pygmies* had started putting their plan into action.

The girls arrived at Grandma Stalberg's house at eight, so there was plenty of time left before the boys would get there. It was raining and the air was unpleasantly cool. But the sky was still bright. First, they had to snatch Huberta and Isolde from the lettuce bed.

"How will I get new lettuce plants before Gran gets back?" Charlie groaned. "And just look at the cabbages!"

"No worries, we'll sort it out," Melanie said. "Can't we take the ones that are left and space them out a bit more?"

Charlie shook her head. "Cabbages have tap-roots. We'll end up killing half of them."

"Ah. Well…" Melanie shrugged.

"You can sometimes buy these little plants from the market," Freya suggested.

Charlie looked around, frowning. "I'd have to buy a whole bunch of those."

"And?" Melanie wiped a big raindrop from her nose. "We'll pool our pocket money. We're a gang, after all. Aren't we?"

"Right," Charlie murmured, and suddenly she felt better.

She gave the others a crooked smile.

"What did your parents say about Grandma Stalberg's clothes?" Freya asked, giggling.

"Oh, the dress!" Melanie slapped her hand on her forehead. "My mum put it in the wash immediately. I'll give it back to you tomorrow."

"My parents totally cracked up when they saw me," Freya said. "I told them we played 'afternoon tea' in those things. But I had to swear that the clothes were from the attic and not from Grandma Stalberg's wardrobe."

"My parents just wrinkled their noses," Trudie muttered. "'You take that off right now!' my dad shouted. 'You're just making yourself look even more frumpy…'" she looked at her feet, "'…than usual.'"

The others stayed silent. Then Freya put her arm around Trudie. "Nonsense!" she said. "He hasn't got a clue anyway. If he knew that you're one of the infamous *Wild Chicks*, he'd think twice about what he says to you."

"Exactly!" Melanie said, linking her arm into Trudie's. "And now, enough standing around in the rain. Time to make Grandma Stalberg's house *Pygmy*-safe, right?"

"Right!" the others shouted.

And Charlie took charge. "First stop—henhouse!"

To make sure the *Pygmies* couldn't release the hens again, Charlie locked the door of the henhouse from the inside.

Then she climbed out through the window and nailed a plank in front of it. The hens were of course already sitting on their perches. On the second strike of the hammer, Mr. Stoutspeck peered over the hedge.

"What are you doing there?" he asked suspiciously. "Hammering after 6 pm is forbidden. A big girl like you should know that!"

"But haven't you heard?" Melanie asked. She was standing by the gate with Freya and Trudie. "There's going to be a storm tonight. One where the cars start flying through the air and stuff. That's why we're nailing up the windows."

"Yes!" Charlie nodded. "You should do the same, Mr. Stoutspeck. And you better not set another foot outside tonight. We're going inside now as well."

Mr. Stoutspeck shot a worried glance at the sky and looked at the grey clouds.

"Doesn't look anything like a storm!" he grumbled. Trudie's lips were twitching. She swallowed a giggle, quickly turned her blushing head away, and ran off toward the shed.

Freya ran after her.

"They said it in the radio?" Mr. Stoutspeck asked.

"Yes!" Charlie whacked the last nail into the plank. It was a little crooked, but the window was secured. "On that special station for homeowners and chicken—and pigeon breeders."

Mr. Stoutspeck had a lot of pigeons. He couldn't stand chickens. Grandma Stalberg always said that one pigeon made more mess than all of her hens combined.

"What's that station? Rubbish!" Mr. Stoutspeck growled. "Never heard of such a radio station."

"Funny," Charlie said. "My gran's always listening to it. Good evening, Mr. Stoutspeck."

Then she ran with Melanie to the garden shed. Freya and Trudie were leaning against Grandma Stalberg's tool shelf, giggling themselves into a frenzy.

"I swear, if he starts nailing up his windows I'll explode!" Trudie panted.

"First he'll probably crank his radio like crazy, to find that special station," said Charlie. She looked around. "Now, what could we use?"

"How about those nets up there?" Melanie asked.

"Yes! The fruit nets." Charlie climbed on to a pile of wooden crates and pulled the nets from the shelf. "That's a good idea. Gran always puts them over the cherry trees, so the birds don't get all the cherries."

"Great!" Melanie grinned with anticipation. "If we get one of them stretched over the path, we could catch the *Pygmies* like fish."

"Hmm!" Charlie's forehead wrinkled up and she rubbed her nose intently. "It's not going to be easy, but let's try. What else could we use?"

"We could dig a trap!" Trudie suggested excitedly. "Right behind the gate, just like they did in Tarzan, you know?"

Charlie rolled her eyes. "Have you ever tried to dig a hole that big? We'd still be digging next week."

"Yeah?…bummer," Trudie mumbled.

"I thought we just wanted to chase the boys away." Freya sat down on a rusty garden chair. "But catching them—" her face lit up, "—is much better!"

"Yes, and the net is perfect, right?" Melanie giggled. "They love fishing, and now they'll be the fish."

The *Wild Chicks* burst out laughing.

"And when we have them, wiggling in the net," Freya wiped tears of laughter from her eyes, "We'll make them a peace offer—noble as we are. So we can look for the treasure in peace. What do you think?"

"Agreed," said Melanie.

"Hmm!" Trudie nodded. "That's good."

Only Charlie didn't look at all happy. "Can't we decide that later?" she grumbled. "First we should set the net, or we'll never catch our fish—and you can forget about your peace deal."

Melanie opened the shed door a crack and looked outside. "You're right, it's getting dark," she said. "We have to hurry."

Outside, the rain was still pouring down.

By the time they had everything ready, they were all soaked to the skin. They had gotten caught in their own net twice, and the darker it got the more often they stumbled over the strings they had tied to the net.

Whether it was the rain, or Charlie's storm-alert, not once did Mr. Stoutspeck's red head appear over the hedge.

Sneezing, and with aching knees, the girls finally ran into the house. They pulled off their soaking clothes and, for the second time that day, fetched clothes from the attic. The strings from the net hung through the open kitchen window.

"Oh no! So we can't shut the window," said Melanie, as she rubbed her hair dry with Grandma Stalberg's towel.

Trudie sneezed so loudly she gave the others a start. "And we can't turn on the light, either," she sniveled.

"Well, if you keep sneezing like that, they'll know we're here anyway," said Charlie. She looked with concern at the lace on the hem of her black dress. "I hope I won't ruin that one as well!" she said. "The one I wore in the forest is totally done for."

"Mine looks quite bad as well," Trudie said sheepishly. "I gave it to my mum, and she asked me whether she shouldn't just throw it away."

Charlie groaned. "Great! Can someone please tell me how to fix the dresses so my gran doesn't notice anything?"

"Well, mine is perfectly fine," Melanie said. "Just has to be washed."

"Give them to me," said Freya. "I'll mend them."

"You can sew?" Trudie asked incredulously. "I mean, for real?"

Freya nodded. "I even made myself a pair of trousers. And clothes for my dolls and stuff. I'll mend the dresses."

Outside, it had grown dark. Just as dark as the night Charlie had searched for Isolde with her mum. The four *Wild Chicks* crowded the kitchen window. Each held one of the strings, which stretched right across Grandma Stalberg's garden and into the fruit trees on both sides of the path. The big net hung, barely visible, in the darkness between the trees.

Charlie shook her head. "That's not going to work," she said quietly. "Two of us have to go outside, under the trees, and pull from there. One left, one right."

"What? Out there?" Melanie frowned. "Well…any volunteers?"

Freya gave Charlie a nudge. "Come on, we'll do it, right?"

"Okay," Charlie nodded. "After all, we're not made of sugar, unlike our sweet Melanie."

"Ha-ha!" Melanie pulled a grimace.

"There's two coats by the door," Charlie said. "We'll put those on."

They were proper grandma coats: thick, dark, and heavy.

"You look great!" Melanie said, giggling. "The boys will think they're being attacked by a couple of loony grans."

"It's already a quarter to nine," Trudie whispered. She pushed her nose against the window pane. "They'll be here soon."

But they still had to wait for a long time.

CHAPTER 15

It was a quarter past ten when the *Pygmies* arrived.

Despite their thick coats, Charlie and Freya were chilled so thoroughly that their teeth were chattering. Their feet were soaking wet from the rain, and the water dripped from their hair down into their collars.

Disgusting.

Why does it have to rain today, of all days? Charlie thought angrily. *Why, why, why?* She was just about to get up, because her legs had fallen asleep and her knees hurt like hell, when she heard the bicycles. The grinding of wheels on the wet gravel, the clattering of mudguards—and boys' voices.

"What shit-weather!" Baz said.

Steve was moaning: "Couldn't we have postponed the whole thing 'til tomorrow?"

Charlie heard how they stopped, dismounted, and leaned their bikes against the hedge.

"Stop whining," Fred said. "The weather is great. At least there's nobody on the streets, or looking at the flowers in their garden. And the whole thing would be done already if Steve kept his bike in better nick."

"Someone's been fiddling with it!" Steve called. "I swear!"

"Yes, whatever!" said Fred. "And now quiet!"

Grandma Stalberg's gate gave a quiet squeak as he opened it. Charlie and Freya pressed themselves as closely as possible against the dripping tree trunks. The boys stopped, hesitating. They looked toward the house.

"It's all dark," Willie whispered.

"Of course!" Fred whispered back. "Nobody's here. And now stop peeing your pants."

They crept toward the house at a snail's speed.

Come on! Charlie thought. A few more steps and they'd be right under the net.

"Hey, Fred!" Steve said. He stopped. "I don't know. You really think we can just go in there?" His voice sounded shrill with agitation.

"Oh, come on," Fred said angrily. "We're not going to break anything, or stuff. And we're not going to steal anything."

"Except for the treasure." Baz giggled nervously.

"But it's still sort of like a burglary," Steve objected.

"Twaddle!" Fred hissed. "We have a key. Do burglars have keys?"

Steve didn't answer. Nobody said anything.

"Come on!" Fred breathed, and the four started moving again.

Now! Charlie thought. Her heart was jumping like a yo yo. She gave a sharp whistle, and the four *Wild Chicks* pulled their strings.

Charlie's whistle made the *Pygmies* freeze into pillars of salt. Grandma Stalberg's fruit net dropped on them like the net of a giant spider. Surprised, they stumbled into each other, got even more tangled up, and finally dropped to the muddy ground like a pile of freshly caught herring.

"Precision work!" Charlie called. She jumped up and together with Freya ran toward the wriggling net. The *Pygmies* were lying on Grandma Stalberg's garden path, cursing and screaming at the top of their voices.

Melanie and Trudie came running out of the house. Trudie pointed a flashlight at their haul. Wet from the rain, the *Pygmies* really did look like very peculiar fish. Two of them managed to get to their knees, and they stared angrily at the girls through the mesh of the net.

"Let us out, now!" Fred cursed.

Giggling, Melanie linked arms with Charlie and Freya. "Well? Didn't we do great?"

"You stupid cows!" Baz barked.

"Really wasn't easy, pulling just at the right moment," Trudie said.

Charlie crouched down and grinned at the fuming Fred. Willie and Steve had meanwhile also managed to scramble to their knees, but they were still speechless with shock. And while Willie had put on his Frankenstein face again, Steve just looked completely puzzled, and a little bit scared.

"Well, you burglars?" Charlie said. "And what shall we do

with you? Any suggestions?"

"It was just for fun," Steve piped. "Just like you did with the ladder."

"That was different," Charlie said.

"How?" Baz asked. He was trying to yank his arm free of Steve's big leg. "What was different about that? Hmm?"

"No police!" Willie suddenly blurted out. It sounded very close to panicky. "Please don't!"

"What gave you that stupid idea?" Charlie asked, annoyed. "I just want my grandma's keys back. Then we'll let you go."

"Just hand them over, Fred!" Baz said.

Fred petulantly tried to reach his trouser pockets, but that wasn't so easy in the jumble of legs and arms.

"Can't reach. No chance. Steve's fat butt is in the way."

"Wait. I'll try," Steve said, and after a few contortions he managed to reach into Fred's pocket. "Got it!"

"Phew, good stuff!" Baz groaned. "Then just give them that thing, finally!" He sneezed. "Damn, now I have a cold. It's your fault!"

"You'll live!" Melanie taunted him. She giggled as she gave Trudie a nudge. "How silly they all look right now! I'll never forget that."

"Damn!" Stevie moaned. "Now I've dropped the keys into the mud."

"If that's another trick…" Charlie said.

"Not a trick. Honest!" Steve protested. He was desperately

digging around in the muddy earth.

"No, he just is that stupid!" Fred growled glumly. "Have you got it? I can't feel my butt anymore."

"Yes, here it is!" Steve called out with relief. He pushed his short, stubby fingers through the net and handed the muddy key ring to Charlie.

"Yuck!" Charlie said, disgusted. "What a mess!"

"Sorry!" Steve grinned sheepishly. "Wasn't on purpose!"

"Shall we let them out now?" Trudie asked.

"Hey, there's a car coming," Willie called out in alarm.

Baffled, Trudie shone her flashlight toward the gate.

There really was a car—checkered blue and yellow, with lights on the roof.

"Police!" Charlie whispered. "What are they doing here?"

"You called them!" Willie shrieked. "You mean cows!" He started yanking at the net in panic. "I have to get out of here!"

"Hey, cool it!" Fred said.

"We did not call them," Charlie assured them. "Word of honor. We're not daft!"

She stared transfixed at the car. The doors opened and two policemen got out.

Melanie pulled at the net. "Come on, help me!" she hissed. Together, the *Wild Chicks* started pulling the net, but the boys had gotten so entangled they couldn't get it off them.

"They're coming in!" Freya whispered.

The policemen opened the gate. One of them was huge

and quite round. The other one was scrawny and short. "Good evening, ladies, gents," the little one said.

"Good evening!" the *Wild Chicks* replied in unison.

"Good evening!" the *Pygmies* muttered from their net.

"Isn't this a little late for you all?" the big policeman asked, casting a surprised look at the filled fruit tree net.

"Oh," Charlie said. "We only have school at ten tomorrow."

"Really?" The two policemen exchanged a grin. "Well, but anyway, what exactly are you doing there, if we may ask?"

The boys looked at the girls pleadingly.

"We're celebrating a little," said Melanie. "You know, it's my birthday. And we were playing some wild games."

"That does look a little wild," said the short policeman. "And what is that game called?"

"Pygmy trap," Freya answered.

"Ah!" The policemen exchanged another glance. The boys had still not uttered a word.

"Could you maybe help us get the net off them?" Trudie asked shyly. "We can't do it."

"Of course!" the two policemen replied, and immediately got to work.

"Did you come here by chance?" Charlie asked.

One leg and one arm of Fred's were already free.

"No, we were called," the big one said, holding up one side of the net. "Right, crawl out through here."

Fred and Baz wriggled to freedom, caked in mud and dripping. Sighing with relief, they got to their feet.

"My arm's still stuck!" Steve whined.

"Wait, we'll sort you out," the little policeman said.

"What do you mean, you were called?" Charlie asked incredulously. "Who called?"

"A Mr. Stoutspeck!" The big one answered while he pulled Steve's arm free. "Right, that just leaves one."

"I'm coming!" Willie said quietly.

"I should have known!" Charlie muttered.

"He complained about 'a disturbance of the peace'," the little policeman explained.

"And he reported an attempted burglary by a gang of youths," the other one added. "But you didn't notice anything, did you?"

The *Wild Chicks* shook their heads emphatically, as did the *Pygmies*.

"Mr. Stoutspeck is bonkers!" Charlie said. "He's always saying such weird things. And he's always spying."

"He lives next door?" the big policeman asked. He produced a notebook.

"Yes, yes," Charlie looked wearily at the notebook. "What are you writing?"

"That it's just routine," the policeman replied. "And we didn't notice anything suspicious around here."

"Oh!" Charlie cast an angry look at Mr. Stoutspeck's

hedge. "Typical. Really typical. He's always got his big nose poking over that hedge, but now he's nowhere to be seen."

"Coward!" Melanie said, giving the two policemen her brightest smile.

"That's how it usually goes," said the little policeman. "The people who call us never show up. Sometimes they don't even give us their name. Well…" he looked at the dripping children, "…who actually lives here?"

"Me," Charlie quickly answered. "And my girlfriends are staying the night."

"Ah. And your parents? Where are they?"

"My mother's still working," Charlie said. Her ears were getting quite hot. "But she'll be here soon, definitely."

"And your father?"

"Don't have one," Charlie answered.

"Fine." The policemen looked at each other. "We couldn't have taken you all anyway. Then we'll just get these gentlemen home."

"What?" The boys' eyes went wide with shock. "But…but we'll get into huge trouble when we turn up with the cop… I mean with the police," Fred stuttered. "My dad will think I did god knows what."

"My dad will kill me," Willie muttered. "He'll just whack me dead."

Charlie rubbed her nose. "I forgot to say," she called out, "The boys are of course also sleeping over, kind of."

"You kind of remembered that quite late," said the small policeman.

"That's just because…because I'm quite tired already!" Charlie replied. She yawned theatrically.

The policemen put their heads together and conferred. One of them looked at his watch. They whispered for quite a while. Then, finally, they turned around again. The children stared at them anxiously.

"Fine," the big one said. "We'll come by here again in an hour. If your mother is not back by then, we'll take the first car load of you home."

"But…"

"No buts. And if we get another call about any noise, then we'll ship you all home immediately. Understood?"

"Understood!" the *Wild Chicks* mumbled.

"Understood!" the *Pygmies* mumbled.

"Right, 'til in an hour, then," the little one said, putting two fingers to his peaked cap. "And meanwhile, try and get some kip."

"Will do," Charlie grumbled.

And the two policemen were gone.

"Is your mum really coming home soon?" Fred asked.

"Not a chance!" Charlie replied glumly. Now she was rubbing her nose like crazy. "And I'm not sure I can get her here in an hour."

CHAPTER 16

"Come on," said Charlie, signaling the whole crowd to follow her. "Let's go into the house first."

"Nope, I'm out of here!" said Willie. "Right now." And he ran off toward the gate.

"Check out what you look like!" Fred called. "You can't turn up at home like that."

"Still better than not turning up at all. What time is it anyway?"

"Eleven." Trudie said. "Quite exactly."

"Oh, shit." Willie climbed quickly on to his bike. The others thought they could hear a sob, but then he was gone, without another word.

"What's with him?" Freya asked with concern.

"His father likes to beat him," Fred explained.

Downcast, they all filed into Grandma Stalberg's kitchen. Charlie turned on the light. She filled the kettle and put it on the stove.

"I think we could all do with something hot," she said.

"Where do your parents think you are?" Melanie asked the boys.

"They think I'm at Fred's," Steve said with a sheepish grin. He looked around Grandma Stalberg's kitchen.

"Mine too," said Baz. He looked down at himself. "Jeez,

look at me. You don't happen to have some dry clothes?" He blushed. "I mean, clothes for boys."

"No, just a whole lot of old dresses!" Trudie chuckled.

Freya eyed the boys from head to toe. "But you have to get out of those things," she said. "Else you'll have a big fat cold tomorrow, or something even worse. Nobody will see you if you put on the dresses here. But whether we can get your things dry by tomorrow…?" She shrugged.

"Then they'll have to wear dresses to school," Melanie said.

Now bright red, the boys looked at their muddy trousers.

"I can turn on the heating," Charlie suggested. "If we hang them over the radiators, they'll be dry by tomorrow. And then we can brush out the mud."

"Thanks!" Fred looked at the others. "Man, I feel as cold as a popsicle."

Freya and Charlie hung their coats up in the hall. When they returned to the kitchen, Fred muttered: "Okay, we'll put on those ridiculous dresses."

"Very sensible of you," said Melanie. "The bathroom is back there. Come on, Trudie, let's check what we have in the attic." The boys quickly disappeared into the bathroom.

"I have to call the taxi service," said Charlie. "They'll need to radio Mum." Sighing, she poured the boiling water into the teapot. "She will be so mad!"

Freya put seven mugs on the table.

"You can put out some biscuits as well," Charlie said.

"Doesn't matter anymore. If I imagine all the stuff Stoutspeck is going to tell my gran. Oh dear."

"Do you have the number of the taxi service?" Freya asked as she put the biscuit tin on the table.

"No, it's at home, of course," Charlie said. "But Gran's phone book is over there in the cupboard. She might have the number in there."

Freya looked through the book. "Here's a *Flash-Taxi*."

"That's it," said Charlie. She went to the phone with pursed lips. She looked very unhappy. "My mum can't stand it when I lie to her," she said. She hesitantly picked up the receiver. "Go on."

"23331," Freya read.

"Right. Now I remember it," Charlie said. "Quite simple, really."

Melanie and Trudie returned with piles of trousers, jumpers, and dresses.

"Psst!" Freya put a finger on her lips. "Charlie's calling her mum."

"Oh no. She's going to flip, isn't she?" Melanie whispered. "We found some old trousers of Charlie's upstairs. They are probably too short, but I bet the boys would rather put on these than the dresses. Come," she nudged Trudie, "Let's put them by the bathroom door."

"Yes, hello?" Charlie breathed into the phone. "This is Charlotte Stalberg…yes, right. Could you give a message to my mum? She shouldn't worry, but could she please come to my gran's house as quickly as possible? Very urgent, yes. Thanks!"

Charlie was as white as a sheet as she put the phone down. "I've never called her at work."

"Crap! Now you're getting all the trouble!" Freya said.

"Well…" Charlie shrugged. "But I tell you one thing: that Mr. Stoutspeck has something coming. Damn, the tea!" She quickly ran to the stove and pulled the strainer out of the teapot. "Pitch black!"

"Your things fit them quite well!" Melanie grinned as she pushed Fred and Baz into the kitchen. "Only Steve was a little more difficult."

Steve came in behind Trudie, his face as red as a tomato. He had squeezed into one of Charlie's t-shirts, and he looked like an overstuffed sausage. The stripy corduroys wouldn't button up, and the girls had cut the trouser legs open all the way to his knees. Fred and Baz, however, fitted perfectly into the things Charlie had long outgrown.

"Quite handy, that you're all such shorties!" Melanie teased them.

"As long as we don't have to wear dresses," Baz muttered.

Charlie poured the tea. She looked nervously at the clock and sat on the edge of her chair, as if ready to jump up any moment. Steve was mesmerized by Grandma Stalberg's biscuits. Trudie took two and pushed one toward him.

"Did you call your mum?" Fred asked.

Charlie nodded, but she couldn't look at him.

"Yeah, great!" Freya said angrily to Fred. "Your parents are never going to hear about the mess you made. But Charlie is going to be in big-time trouble with her mum."

"We're sorry," Baz mumbled. "Really. But how is it our fault your stupid neighbor called the police?"

"And how is it *our* fault?" Melanie flicked her hair back. "Who started with all this crap?"

"Not us!" Fred called out, outraged.

"Of course, you!" Charlie called. "Who let out the chickens?"

Steve stared at his fingers, but then he just couldn't control himself any longer. He took another biscuit.

"And what about the ladder?" Baz asked. "How was that fair?"

"That was just revenge for the chickens," Melanie retorted. "And then you locked us into Mouseman's shed."

"And you fiddled with our bikes!" Fred shouted angrily.

"And you?" Charlie slammed the table with her palm so hard that the tea spilled out of all the mugs. "You stole my keys. And then you were going to break in. If that isn't mean, then I don't know what is."

"That's all complete bull," Fred muttered. "Complete rubbish, from start to finish."

At that moment, the doorbell rang. They all looked

anxiously at the clock, and Charlie turned as white as Grandma Stalberg's teapot. She got up slowly, as if her legs had turned to lead.

The doorbell rang again. And again.

Charlie opened the door.

"Hi Mum," she said miserably. "Thanks for coming."

For a long moment, Charlie's mum just looked at her daughter. Then she grabbed her by the shoulders and spun her around. She sighed with relief. "You look quite intact," she said incredulously. "What in heaven's name are you doing here, Charlotte? I thought you were at Freya's."

"That…that was a lie," Charlie stuttered. "Because… because…I just had to, Mum. Because…"

"Because what?" her mother asked crossly. "You never lie to me."

"Oh, please, Mum!" Charlie pleaded. "I'll explain everything. Promise. But that'll take too long now, because…" she took a deep breath without looking at her mother, "…the police will be here any moment."

"Wha—? The police? Why the police?" her mother asked, appalled. "For heaven's sake, just tell me what's going on."

Charlie took her hand. "Just come in first, Mum. Then I'll explain. It's complicated, you know." With a sheepish smile, she pulled her mother into the kitchen.

"Those are all my friends, Mum," she said. "More or less."

Dumbfounded, her mother took in the group around the

kitchen table.

"Good evening, Ms. Stalberg," said Melanie. "So nice of you to come."

"Evening," Fred mumbled under his breath.

"Evening," Baz and Steve chimed in.

"Why are the boys wearing your old clothes?" Charlie's mother asked breathlessly. "And what are you all doing here at this time of night?" With a big sigh she dropped into Charlie's chair. "God, I have to sit down. I ran at least ten red lights to get here as quickly as possible. And what do I find? A children's party!" She shook her head and looked at Charlie. "You can be glad your gran's not here to see this."

"Do you want tea?" Charlie asked meekly. "It's blackberry. Your favorite."

Her mother nodded.

"Mum, the police are going to come back soon," Charlie said, putting a mug of tea in front of her mother. "Could you tell them that they are all allowed to sleep over here tonight, because we had a party?"

"Ah," Charlie's mother said. "You had a party. And what did you celebrate? Or is that another one of your top secret thingies?"

"We didn't really have a party," Freya explained. "That's just what we told them, you know?"

Charlie's mother shook her head. "To be quite honest, I'm not sure what I know anymore."

"Never mind, Ms. Stalberg," Melanie said soothingly. "As long as the police see that there's an adult here now, they'll be okay."

"Uh-huh?" Charlie's mum muttered. "But I'm not okay. At all. What did you get up to, that the police had to turn up here?"

"Really, nothing bad," Charlie said. "Not at all. But that nosy Mr. Stoutspeck ratted us out."

"Ratted you out? What, in heaven's name for?"

"Charlie," Freya interjected. "I think you have to explain this all from scratch. Otherwise your mum won't understand a word."

"Fine," Charlie sighed. "If you think so. About the treasure as well?"

Freya nodded.

Charlie's mum groaned. "What treasure?"

Charlie rubbed her nose. "Gran's treasure, Mum," she said. "I better get started, or else the police will come back and you'll have no idea what to tell them."

"Right, then," Charlie's mother said, after having learned the whole complex story about the *Wild Chicks* and the *Pygmies*. "I'll sort this out for you. But under one condition."

"Here it comes," Baz muttered.

Charlie's mum continued. "I want you all to make peace. Right here, at this table. We don't know how long that peace may last, but those are my terms."

The *Wild Chicks* looked at the *Pygmies*, and the *Pygmies* looked at the *Wild Chicks*.

Finally, Fred spoke. "We need to discuss this."

"So do we," said Charlie.

"Fine, discuss," her mother said. "But you don't have much time."

And so Charlie, Freya, Melanie, and Trudie stuck their heads together on one side of Grandma Stalberg's table, and Fred, Baz, and Steve did the same on the other side.

Finally Charlie lifted her head. "We agree," she announced. "Anyway, we've got better things to do than all this back-and-forth stuff."

"We agree as well," Fred said. "And we're saying this also in Willie's name. Peace."

"Unless you start bugging us again," Baz said.

"What? Us?" Charlie asked. "It's still you who started all this."

"Are we at it again already?" Charlie's mother interrupted.

The kids looked contritely at Grandma Stalberg's flowery tablecloth.

"No," Charlie mumbled. "Peace."

"Peace," Fred repeated. He held his hand out across the table.

Charlie took it. Melanie, Freya, Trudie, Baz, and Steve all piled their hands on top.

"Great," Charlie's mum said. "Then I think we're ready for the police!"

CHAPTER 17

harlie's mother acquitted herself perfectly with the police. She told them she'd only been gone a short while to take a child who had wanted to go home, but now she was back, and would the officers like to come in for a cup of coffee? The small policeman and the big one declined politely and drove off, satisfied. And Fred muttered something about how one could easily envy Charlie her mother. The others agreed readily. And Charlie was so proud she nearly exploded!

Then they tried to work out how the four *Wild Chicks* and the three *Pygmies* could all find a place to sleep in Grandma Stalberg's little house. None of them could go home, of course, or they would have blown each other's cover stories.

In the end, Charlie slept in Grandma Stalberg's bed with her mum. Melanie and Trudie shared the bed in which Charlie usually slept, and Freya slept on the sofa in the kitchen—which she declared to be amazingly comfortable. The boys spent the night in the attic, where, with some help from the girls, they build a first-class mega-bed from old carpets, knitting cushions and blankets. The *Pygmies* had to swear by the honor of their gang that they would not do any snooping around in Grandma Stalberg's stuff.

But after the rest of the house had long gone to sleep, Charlie could still hear giggles and whispers above her head. *What if they don't stick to their promise?* she thought, and she pondered whether she shouldn't sneak up there and check, just to be sure. But she was fast asleep before she could even get one leg out from under the duvet.

The *Pygmies* kept their promise. Grandma Stalberg's boxes and crates did look untouched when the girls came in the next morning to wake the boys. "Breakfast!" Charlie screamed as loud as she could, before she stormed up the ladder with the others. Three very sleepy faces emerged from Grandma Stalberg's knitting cushions.

"Yes, yes!" Fred mumbled, forcing open one puffy eye. "What's the time?"

"Six!" Melanie announced. Without further ado, she pulled the blanket off the boys. "Charlie's hens have been up for hours."

"And we already fed them," Freya said, tickling Steve's naked foot. Snickering, he quickly hid under his blanket.

"Six o'clock?" Baz howled. "Have you gone mad? I get up at seven thirty, and not a minute earlier. Seven thirty—is that clear?"

"Of course you can do that," said Charlie. "*If* you want to go to school in my clothes."

Baz stared at her in shock. "Why? Aren't our things dry yet?"

Melanie laughed. "Dry, yes," she said. "But also rock hard with mud."

"Yep, brushing them out won't do any good," Freya added. "That's why we thought you might want to go home to get changed. But if you'd rather sleep a little more…" she shrugged.

"Yes, if they'd rather sleep a bit more," Charlie chimed in, pulling Melanie and Freya toward the ladder. "Then we should let them, right?"

Giggling, the four girls climbed down the ladder.

"All right, all right!" Fred shouted after them. "We're coming!"

And the boys quickly squeezed themselves into the far-too-short trousers.

After breakfast—which turned out to be quite a raucous and fun affair—the *Pygmies* disappeared as quickly as firemen. The *Wild Chicks* generously offered to wash up, so the boys could get their hands on trousers that actually fit. With the help of Charlie's mother, they erased at least the most obvious traces the seven children had left behind in Grandma Stalberg's house. It was a lot of work, and so the *Wild Chicks*, just like the *Pygmies*, just about managed to get to school before the first bell.

The boys were as red as cherries as they parked their bikes next to the girls'.

"Go ahead," Fred said to Charlie. He was nervously chewing his lip. "We—ehm—we'll catch up with you."

"Yes!" Baz added.

Steve stared at his friends, dumbfounded. "Why? I thought we made peace last night!" he called out.

"Sure!" Fred said sheepishly. "But we still don't have to be together all the time, right?"

"What?" Freya gasped. "We just had breakfast together and now you're already starting with that silly stuff again?"

"Just leave those idiots be!" Charlie said. "They're just afraid their mates will laugh about them if they come marching into class with us girls. I get it. Come on, we're out of here."

They all turned their backs on the *Pygmies* and went off toward the front steps.

"Maybe we should tell their friends how we trapped them last night," Melanie said over her shoulder. "That'll give them something to laugh about."

"You can't do that!" Baz shouted after them.

But the girls were already through the front door.

"Jeez, last night I bent over backwards for them, and nearly messed things up with my mum," Charlie complained. "I'm such a fool."

"Hey, Charlie, wait a second!" Fred called.

They caught up with the girls by the assembly hall.

"Don't get all huffy," Fred said, trying to keep pace with

Charlie's long legs. "I didn't mean it like that."

"Sure you did!" Charlie retorted. "And now you're just afraid we might tell the others what happened last night."

"Not true!" Fred shouted indignantly.

They stopped in front of their classroom, the girls on one side, the boys on the other.

"Yes, true!" Charlie hissed. She opened the door. "I'm going in now. You can stand out here for a few more minutes, just to be safe."

"Exactly!" said Melanie. And the *Wild Chicks* disappeared into the classroom, just as Mrs. Rose was coming down the corridor.

"Oh dear, what's bitten you?" she asked when she saw the expression on the boys' faces.

"Chickens," said Fred. "A big bunch of wild chicks."

"Got another one!" Freya whispered, pushing a folded up note toward Charlie.

"Give it to me," Charlie growled.

"Willie still isn't here," Freya whispered.

"I don't care," Charlie hissed back. She unfolded the note.

Mrs. Rose had ordered Elizabeth, her star pupil, to the blackboard. Mrs. Rose was beaming like a Cheshire cat about so much mathematical talent. And the rest of the class had their peace for a while.

"Let me see," Freya said, peering over Charlie's shoulder.

Second peace offering, it said in Fred's terrible scrawl. Underneath, he had drawn three heads. And then: *What are you doing on the weekend? How about a peace party? We buy the food. Word of honer. The Pygmies.*

"Honor without an o. Oh dear," Freya muttered.

Charlie had, of course, not noticed that.

"Come on." Freya gave her friend a nudge. "We'll write back. Yes?"

"We have to discuss this with the others first," Charlie whispered. Elizabeth had already filled half the blackboard with her neat little numbers.

"Send Melanie Fred's note, and write on it that they should nod if they agree."

"Hmmm—alright, fine!" Charlie said. She scribbled the message underneath that of the boys, and tapped on Paula's shoulder in front of her.

"To Melanie!" she hissed. Paula nodded grudgingly and passed Charlie's note on. Sadly, at that very moment Elizabeth went back to her seat, and Mrs. Rose looked over the classroom.

"Damn!" Freya whispered.

Mrs. Rose was the most notorious note-hunter in the whole school, and of course this note did not escape her eagle-eyes.

"Oh!" she said, pursing her lips. "What's that, making its way across my classroom? Paula, please show it to me."

Paula ruefully handed her the note.

"Ah, an invitation," Mrs. Rose announced. "I'll just pass this on verbally, shall I, Charlie?"

"Okay," Charlie mumbled, staring at the table top.

"Well, Melanie and Trudie, you're supposed to nod if you agree to celebrate a peace party with the *Pygmies* this weekend. The gentlemen will provide food. Hmm. A peace party." Mrs Rose pouted. "That is the nicest piece of news I have ever intercepted. And the most pleasing. Go on, you two. Nod!"

Melanie and Trudie grinned, and nodded.

The whole classroom was giggling.

The three *Pygmies* sat there, their heads bright red, and didn't know where to look.

The rest of the class went by without any particular incidents, except that Trudie and Steve were called to the blackboard. Ten minutes before recess, however, there was a knock on the door and Willie came skulking in.

"Oh my god, what does he look like?" Freya whispered in shock.

"Sorry, Mrs. Rose," Willie said quietly. "But I wasn't feeling well this morning. My mother has written a note for you." His head bowed, he put the envelope on the teacher's desk.

"Look at me, William," Mrs. Rose said. "What happened to your face, hmm?"

Willie's left eye was blue and swollen, and his face looked puffy from crying.

Fred turned as white as the wall. Baz's eyes were wide open with shock, and Steve's lower lip began to tremble.

"William!" Mrs. Rose said. "What happened to your face? Answer me, please."

Willie sat down on his seat and covered his eye with his hand. "It's all in the letter," he said. "I fell from my bike."

"Fell from your bike? Right!" Mrs. Rose nodded. "Would you please come to me after this period, Willie? There's something I would like to discuss with you."

A deathly silence had fallen over the classroom.

"What for?" Willie asked. "There's nothing to discuss." His voice sounded nervous. He still had his hand pressed over his eye. "Just ask the others. I had to get home quickly last night and that's when I fell. Can happen to anyone, can't it?"

"Of course, Willie," Mrs. Rose said. She had turned a little pale around the nose. "And you don't have to get worked up. I would just like to have a word later. That's all."

"But I don't want to have a word." Willie's face now actually looked angry.

"Fine." Mrs. Rose shrugged. "Then we won't." And very quietly she added, "But then I won't be able to help you."

"I don't need anybody to help me!" Willie said loudly.

"All right." Mrs. Rose pulled Charlie's and Fred's invitation from her jacket pocket. "Here. This is an invitation that's probably also meant for you. You do belong to the *Pygmies,* don't you?"

Willie nodded, surprised, and he read the note.

"At least you're no longer bashing each other's heads in," Mrs. Rose said. She adjusted her glasses and went back to her desk. "That's a relief, though just a small one."

CHAPTER 18

The peace party was planned for three in the afternoon, at the *Pygmies'* treehouse. The *Wild Chicks*, however, already met in the morning. Right after breakfast, they went to the market together. Charlie wanted to buy some new lettuce and cabbage plants, so that Grandma Stalberg wouldn't have too much to complain about on her return.

"Man, I have no idea how I'm supposed to get all that done before Monday," Charlie groaned as they cycled back to her gran's house with their loaded shopping bags. "There are already more weeds than veggies growing on the beds, and I still have to clean the house. Oh, and the fruit net. It's completely torn. And I have to wash all the clothes, and…"

"We haven't solved the mystery of the black key either," Melanie said. "Or have you forgotten about that?"

"No way, of course not. But I have absolutely no idea where else we could look."

"You know what?" Freya said as they turned into the small street where Grandma Stalberg lived. "Maybe the boys could come tomorrow and help. They do kind of owe you, after all. And there isn't much they can mess up plucking weeds."

Trudie giggled. "And they're afraid of chickens anyway."

Laughing, they all parked their bikes.

Charlie looked around. "Oh dear," she said, "This really looks bad."

The fruit net was still lying on the path, and her grandma's flowerbeds looked quite worse for wear. "Phew," Melanie sighed. "I wouldn't even know where to start. I think we can forget about our treasure hunt."

"Hey, look who's coming!" Freya said suddenly.

Fred, Baz, and Steve were cycling down the street. Their bikes were also loaded to capacity with shopping bags.

Charlie frowned. "What are they doing here? That's really the last thing I need."

"Hey!" Fred said as he stopped his bike in front of Grandma Stalberg's gate. "Surprised?"

"Yes, we are," Charlie growled suspiciously. "What are you doing here?"

"Fred thought you could do with a little help," Baz said.

"With what? Finding the treasure?" Charlie asked.

"Bah, that treasure of yours doesn't exist anyway," Fred jeered. "But your gran's coming back Monday and we thought…"

"And how do you know that?" Charlie asked.

"Trudie told us!" Steve answered.

"I…I thought we're at peace now," Trudie stuttered.

"And? That doesn't mean we have to tell them everything, does it?"

"Oh, Charlie, come on," Melanie said. "Don't be such a grouch. It's nice of them to want to help us. Where is Willie?"

"He's coming to the treehouse in the afternoon," Fred mumbled.

For a moment, nobody said anything.

Then Freya opened the gate.

"Come in. What's all the stuff you brought?"

"Oh, most of it is for this afternoon," Baz said, dragging the first couple of bags through the gate. "It cost us half our gang funds."

"But those are lettuce plants and stuff," Trudie observed with surprise.

"Yep. Fred dug them up at his grandpa's," Steve said. "Because…" he grinned sheepishly, "…we might have accidentally trampled a few things around here."

Fred stood and looked at Grandma Stalberg's vegetable beds. "Jeez, that looks bad," he observed expertly, "Quite a bit of work here, I'd say."

"Why?" Charlie asked. "What do you know about it?"

"I do! My grandpa also has a garden like this. No chickens, though. He always gets his manure from the neighbors."

"Ah," Charlie muttered. She looked quite thrown. "And what about the other two?"

"You better let them clean the house," said Fred. "They can't tell a cabbage from a dandelion."

"All right!" Charlie nodded. "We could also use some help

fixing the net."

"Of course!" said Baz. "I'll do that. Anything, as long as I don't have to clean."

"I don't mind cleaning," Steve said.

"Well, then you're with me!" said Melanie. "Us two will tackle the house."

"Me too!" said Trudie. She trundled after the other two. Freya and Baz disappeared into the shed with the torn net. And Charlie and Fred were alone in the garden.

"Right, then!" Charlie said, rubbing her nose. "How many plants did you bring?"

"Fifteen," said Fred. "Five white cabbages, five lettuces and five icebergs."

"Let's have a look."

Proudly, Fred fetched two bags from his bike and put the small plants on the ground in front of Charlie.

"They look nice and strong," Charlie said approvingly. Fred blushed.

"Raised them from seed myself," he said. "Cabbage is really difficult."

"It is," said Charlie. "Last year my gran had maggots in all the roots. Disgusting."

"I had those once," Fred said. "But this year they're all doing fine."

"You know what?" Charlie fetched her own shopping bag. "Compared to yours, the ones from the market are quite pathetic. We should just give those to the hens."

"Fine," said Fred. Together they ran to the chicken run and threw the plants over the fence. The hens attacked the fresh greens with loud clucks.

"Look at that!" Fred chuckled. "They're really fighting over those things."

"Yes, hens are never very nice to each other," Charlie said. "But they're still quite funny."

"They are!" Fred laughed. "Look how they're running. Really looks too ridiculous."

"Whenever I'm in a bad mood," Charlie said, "I just have to look at the hens. You just have to laugh at them!"

"My grandpa doesn't want any," said Fred. "He says they attract rats."

"He's probably right," said Charlie. "I sometimes think my gran only got the chickens to annoy her neighbor, Mr. Stoutspeck." They walked to the water barrel and filled two watering cans with the murky water.

"Is he the one who called the police?" Fred asked.

They carefully placed the plants on the soil, right where the hens had devoured everything, and where Steve and Baz had trampled the plants.

"Yep!" Charlie nodded. "He's a real piece of work."

"Has he got a big red head?" Fred asked in a whisper.

"He does, why?" Charlie was carefully digging small holes for the plants.

"Well, that's the kind of head that's just now looking over the hedge."

Charlie looked up. "Good morning, Mr. Stoutspeck!" she called. "Have the police been to see you?"

"Why?" Mr. Stoutspeck squinted suspiciously.

"For making a false report to the police," said Charlie. "And for insulting an officer. That's what they called it, right, Fred?"

Fred nodded. "Right. That's what they said."

Fred kept the straightest face on earth as he poured water into the plant holes and placed his cabbage plants in Grandma Stalberg's black soil.

"You nasty little brats!" Mr. Stoutspeck panted, and his red head disappeared again behind the hedge.

"Does your grandpa also have nasty neighbors?" Charlie asked.

"No, thank god!" Fred said. He placed the lettuce plants so that their round green leaves lay loosely on the soil.

"Wow, you really know what you're doing," Charlie said admiringly. "I always plant lettuce too deep."

Fred grinned bashfully. "It took me a while, too. But I've been helping my granddad nearly every weekend since my gran died."

"My grandpa has been dead forever," said Charlie. "My gran never talks about him. She doesn't even have a picture of him."

"And your other grandpa?" Fred asked. He wiped the soil from his hands.

"I don't have another one," Charlie said, pursing her lips.

"We need more water," Fred said quickly. "Those lettuces back there look quite droopy."

"I made tea!" Melanie called through the kitchen window. "Super posh. Rose petal. You can all come in!"

Charlie got up. "I'll tell Freya and Baz."

"I'll just put those two in," said Fred. "And then I'll come in. Can you fill the can once more?"

Charlie nodded. She took the empty watering can and walked to the rain barrel. A bee had fallen into the water and was struggling for its life. Charlie carefully fished her out with a leaf. "It's your lucky day!" she mumbled. She filled the can and ran over to the shed. When she got closer, she heard loud giggling.

"Have you heard this one?" she heard Baz say. "A Martian arrives at the airport…"

Charlie opened the battered door. "Hey, you two. Tea's ready," she said.

Baz and Freya were sitting on turned-over crates, the fruit net on their knees.

"Coming!" said Baz. "My side is done anyway."

Freya shook her head and chuckled. "Mine isn't, because he keeps telling me silly jokes. I'm already in stitches."

CHAPTER 19

Grandma Stalberg's kitchen was ready for her return. Melanie had polished the windows and Steve had wiped the floors. Entry was now granted only to those wearing socks. The shoes stayed, neatly lined up, outside the front door. According to Fred, that meant the kitchen soon smelled more of stinky feet than of rose tea, but at least Grandma Stalberg's floor stayed clean.

The boys weren't too convinced by Grandma Stalberg's rose tea. After a few sips, they quickly produced a huge Coke bottle from one of their shopping bags. Trudie stared at it longingly, and so she also got a glass.

"You don't have to clean upstairs," Charlie said to Melanie as she stirred honey into her tea. "I'll take care of that tomorrow."

"How many rooms does this house have?" Baz asked. "Looks quite small from the outside."

"It is small," said Melanie. "The best thing about it is the attic."

"Did you look for the treasure there?" Fred asked.

"Of course!" Charlie pushed her chair up to the cupboard and climbed on it. "Gran always hides some biscuits up there. Yup, here's another tin. Seems to be full."

"Won't you get into trouble if we eat all those as well?" Freya asked anxiously.

Charlie shrugged. "I'm in trouble anyway!" she said, putting the tin on the table. "My gran always finds something to complain about. Now she'll at least have a real reason. And anyway, I helped baking them all."

"Yum!" Melanie said as Charlie opened the lid. "Almond cookies!"

"Yuck!" Steve screamed. He jumped up as if he'd been bitten by a snake. "A spider. A mega-huge spider!"

"Where?" Charlie asked.

"On my lap!" Steve whined. "It landed on my lap. Yuck. There. Now it's on my sleeve."

He flapped his arms around madly, and promptly swiped the teapot from the table. The hot tea splattered all over the kitchen. Charlie just managed to jump aside, but Melanie was hit by a big splash, and then the pot landed under the table, pouring its content all over the rug.

"Damn!" Melanie quickly ran to the tap and ran cold water over her arm.

"Sorry!" Steve whimpered. "But it just sailed from up there right on to me. Just like that."

"And? Where is it now?" Charlie asked, looking at the mess under the table.

"Don't know!" Steve replied.

"Doesn't matter. We have lots of spiders here anyway,"

Charlie mumbled. She fished the pot out of the tea puddle and put it back on the table.

Steve looked around in panic. "Lots?" he stuttered.

"The rug is soaked!" Charlie observed. "Hand me a rag. Quick!"

"Here," said Melanie. "But you'll have to rub it hard—tea stains are a real bummer."

"I know," Charlie muttered from under the table. "Damn! And just as everything was so nice and clean."

"After you're done wiping, we better hang it in the sun," said Freya. "Come on," she gave the boys a nudge. "Help me move the table and the chairs."

"God, there's no end to our labors!" Baz moaned while he and Fred moved the table.

"That'll do!" said Charlie. "Can someone help me roll this thing up?"

Melanie knelt next to her.

"Look at that!" she called out. A hatch had appeared beneath the rolled-up carpet. A hatch in Grandma Stalberg's kitchen floor.

"Looks like a trapdoor or something," said Fred.

Excited, they quickly rolled up the rug a bit more.

"The treasure!" Trudie whispered. "We finally found it!"

"Let's wait and see," said Melanie. "Who knows what's down there." But she had also grown quite white around her nose.

In a combined effort, Charlie and Fred opened the heavy wooden lid. A pitch black hole yawned at them. A narrow and rickety ladder led into the darkness. Dust lay on its rungs, like grey candy floss.

"That's it! Definitely. Very definitely!" Steve piped. He was so excited he nearly fell into the hole. Fred just managed to grab his belt.

"Watch it!" he growled. "You want to break your overeager neck?"

"Wow!" Baz leaned over Charlie's shoulder. "It's probably swarming with rats down there."

Trudie and Steve gave him a terrified look.

"Nonsense!" Charlie sneered. "They would have starved down there ages ago."

Baz shook his head. "Rats never starve. They always find something, even if they have to eat each other."

Melanie screwed her face in disgust. The others looked apprehensively into the dark hole.

"Well, you're welcome to stay up here," Charlie said. "I'll call you when I find the treasure." And with that, she put her foot on the ladder.

"Wait!" Melanie grabbed her arm. "What are you going to do down there without a flashlight?" She looked at the others. "Does anyone have one?"

Shaking heads all around.

"Gran has one in her drawer," Charlie impatiently gestured

toward the cupboard. Fred got up and fetched it.

"Then we can get going, finally," Charlie yanked her arm free and disappeared into the darkness. Fred listened until she had reached the bottom, then he followed her. Melanie was next, then Baz.

"Is there any space left down there?" Steve called down the ladder.

"Are you joking?" Baz called back.

Steve looked at Freya and grinned sheepishly.

"Well, then," he said. And the two of them also climbed down into Grandma Stalberg's hidden cellar.

There were no rats. Just spider webs as big as bath towels and, in a corner, a chest and some half rotten suitcases.

"Oh man, I think my heart just stopped!" Trudie whispered. "The treasure."

"Woohoo!" Steve groaned. "A real, solid, treasure."

"Gold!" Baz whispered. "Silver. Diamonds."

"Don't even think for a moment you're getting a share," said Melanie. "That's our treasure. Is that clear?"

"Why?" Baz asked angrily. "If Steve hadn't tipped over that teapot you would have never found that hatch."

"Shut up, Baz," said Fred. "The treasure belongs to the girls."

Baz pouted his lips.

The seven kids carefully crept toward the chest—as if they

expected a ghost to appear behind it any moment. That, or a flock of crazed bats. But nothing happened.

The chest must have been there for ages. The thick dust on its lid looked like dirty snow.

Charlie produced the bunch of keys, which was still caked with mud, and picked the black key. She carefully scraped the dried earth from its teeth. The others chewed their lips or their fingernails.

"And what if there's a corpse in there?" Steve asked nervously.

"Bull, you old scaredy-cat!" Baz chuckled. "We'd definitely smell that by now. But maybe there's a vampire in there, sleeping—and aaaargh!" He grabbed poor Steve by the throat. "He'll bite us all as soon as we open that chest."

"Let me go!" Steve croaked.

"Stop that!" Fred said crossly.

Charlie knelt in front of the chest and put the black key in its lock. It was quite rusty. Fred pointed the flashlight at the chest.

"The key fits!" Charlie whispered. The others moved in closer.

"Hey, I can't breathe here!" Charlie said. "Everybody—one step back!"

The others obeyed reluctantly.

Charlie turned the key and the lock snapped open. Charlie carefully lifted the heavy lid. Fred quickly pointed his light into the chest.

Two faces were looking back at them. A photograph. A big wedding portrait in a tarnished silver frame. The couple was still very young. The groom had a blonde moustache, and a very serious mouth beneath it. He was wearing a uniform. The woman was smiling. The two of them looked at the children as if they'd been waiting for the chest to finally be opened.

"Treasure? As if!" Baz said disappointedly. "Not even a vampire. Just a dull picture."

The others said nothing. The people in the photograph looked at them. Charlie carefully picked up the picture. "That's my gran!" she muttered.

"And your grandpa, I guess!" said Fred.

Charlie let her finger run over the faces. "I've never seen a picture of him," she said quietly. "He looks just like my mum."

She put the photograph on her lap and leaned over the chest.

"A wedding dress," she said breathlessly, stroking the rustling fabric. It felt quite stiff. "And suits, and shirts, and socks. There's even a pair of shoes. And…" she lifted one of the suits. Moth balls rolled out of the pockets. "…There are letters underneath. Tied up with ribbons."

"Love letters," Melanie whispered.

"Oi…let's have a look, then," said Baz. He reached toward the yellowed envelopes.

"Get your hands off!" Charlie shoved his hand away. "Those are none of your business."

"Ouch!" Baz griped. "Don't be such a ninny!"

"Leave her alone!" Melanie hissed. "Jerk!"

The others retreated quietly.

But Charlie got up and put the photograph back in the chest. She closed the lid, put the black key back in the lock, and locked it.

"Come," she said. "Let's go back up."

"Don't you want to look in those suitcases?" Trudie asked cautiously.

Charlie shook her head. She headed back to the ladder. "That's none of our business," she said firmly.

CHAPTER 20

Ever since she had opened the chest, Charlie felt strange. And that feeling did not go away after she had hidden Grandma Stalberg's secret underneath the kitchen rug again. She could barely say a word. Her head was full of addled thoughts about the wedding couple in the photograph. She felt ashamed. Ashamed for the two who'd been stared at by so many strange eyes. It drove her crazy. In her mind she kept seeing the young woman who had so mysteriously transformed into Grandma Stalberg.

The others noticed what was going on with Charlie. Not a word was spoken about the supposed treasure. Not even by Baz. They cleared the table, washed the dishes, and then they left the brooding Charlie alone at the kitchen table. The boys soon disappeared to prepare everything for the party. "We're still celebrating, aren't we?" Fred asked. "Even without treasure?"

"Of course," Melanie said. They all looked at Charlie.

"Of course," she mumbled.

And then Melanie and Trudie drove home for lunch, and Charlie and Freya were alone.

"Don't you want to go home to eat?" Charlie asked.

Freya shook her head. "If it's okay with you, I'll stay here."

"Okay," Charlie said. "I don't really want to be alone now anyway." She looked at Freya thoughtfully. "You know, in the photo she looked so different, like…" Charlie shrugged.

"Nice," said Freya. "She looks nice. Not at all uptight."

"Yes." Charlie nodded. She got up. "Come on, let's get some eggs and potatoes and make ourselves some lunch."

Together they walked to the henhouse. The vegetable beds looked quite presentable again, thanks to Fred's plants.

"Do you think we'll also turn into grandmas like mine?" Charlie asked as they picked four eggs from the nests. The hens came scrambling in from the run to beg for food.

Freya shrugged, stroking the wings of one of the hens. They felt strange and hard.

"Well, I hope we won't!" Charlie sighed. Then they went back to Grandma Stalberg's kitchen and prepared fried eggs and potatoes with fresh chives.

When Charlie and Freya got to the *Pygmies'* treehouse, Melanie and Trudie were already there. Their legs were dangling peacefully next to those of the boys. Loud radio music boomed through the forest.

"Hey!" Charlie called out as she and Freya climbed the rickety ladder. "Will it get too cramped up there if we come up as well?"

Fred appeared at the top of the ladder, a huge chips bag in one hand, a glass of Coke in the other. "Rubbish!" he said. "Or do you think we built our HQ smaller than your chicken coop?"

"It's quite high!" Charlie observed once she had reached the top. She got a little dizzy looking down. As a precaution she took another step back and sat down on the bench the boys had installed around the trunk of the tree. She had no idea how the others could just sit there and dangle their legs over the edge. At least Freya was feeling the same, and she sat down next to her friend.

"Don't you want to check out the great view?" Melanie asked over her shoulder. "I could scoot over a little."

"No, thanks!" Charlie said. Freya shook her head.

"Ha! Wanna bet? Those two are afraid of heights!" Baz shook himself with laughter.

"Well, chickens aren't really at home on trees!" Steve piped.

"Stop it already!" Fred growled. He held his chips bag out to Charlie.

"No, thanks!" Charlie said.

"Do you want chocolate?" Fred asked. "Or gummy-crocodiles? We've got those, too. They taste totally awful, especially the red ones."

Charlie shook her head. "No, really. Maybe later." Oh god, she was feeling so sick!

"I'd love one of those gummy-crocs," Freya said.

"Sure!" said Fred. "Coming right up. Hey, Steve, give us the bag with the crocs. Or have you eaten them all?"

"Me?" Steve said. He handed them a big paper bag full of

slimy gummy-crocodiles.

"Hey, Fred. Maybe we should have gotten a few bags of chicken feed," Baz said, setting himself laughing again.

"Yes, and we're sorry we forgot the peanuts and bananas, you ape!" said Charlie. She desperately tried to avoid looking over the edge of the platform. Instead, she inspected the inside of the treehouse.

"And? How do you like our *Pygmy* HQ?" Fred asked. "Quite something, isn't it?"

"Hmm." Charlie nodded. "Not bad. Where did you get all this stuff?"

"From the scrapyard, of course," Fred replied. He poured two large mugs of Coke for her and Freya. "They've got everything, and it's just lying around. Carpets, planks, we even found the radio there. Just needed new batteries."

"Do you have to spill about the scrapyard? That's our territory."

"No worries, we have our own sources," Charlie replied pertly. The Coke worked wonders on her stomach. And this place wasn't so bad, as long as she didn't look down.

"We should have an HQ like this," said Melanie. She got up.

"Oh yes!" said Trudie. "Let's do that. But where?"

"We shouldn't discuss that right away," said Charlie. "And I think I do want one of those crocs now."

Fred threw one of the sticky things into her lap.

"What? I thought we made peace!" Steve protested.

"Leave it," Willie grumbled. He went over to the radio and cranked the dial. "We'll find out soon enough."

Baz snickered. "Right!"

"We'll see about that," said Charlie.

Melanie planted herself in front of Fred and held out her plastic cup. "Can I have another drink, or what?"

"Ehm, what? Oh…of course." Fred's ears flushed bright red and he poured her another drink. Then he turned around and yelled, "Hey, Willie! Turn that radio down, will you? Or we'll be deaf soon."

Willie threw him one of his sinister Frankenstein looks, but he did turn down the volume. Baz poured some popcorn into a flowery plastic bowl and put it down in front of the girls. Then he plonked himself next to Freya and slurped his Coke.

"What's with Willie?" Freya whispered to him. "Is it because of his…?" She pointed discreetly at her eye.

Baz shook his head. "No, he just hates having girls up here," he whispered back. "Isn't that right, Willie?" he added, more loudly. "Right? Girls are usually banned from up here."

"Right," Willie growled. He was frowning down at the pond.

Steve giggled and pulled his cards from his pocket.

"Can't we have some other music?" Melanie asked. "That bass is turning my brain to mush."

"Oh yes, girly-whirly music," Willie growled again. "I think I better be off."

"No, we're off," Baz said, cranking the radio. "We're going dancing."

"Dancing? Up here?" Melanie giggled, immediately earning herself an exasperated look from Charlie.

"Rubbish. Down there, of course," Baz said. "How about it? Who's game?"

A few minutes later Baz, Melanie, Steve, and Freya were bouncing around the pond like crazy. Trudie was sitting next to the glumly silent Willie. She looked longingly at the fun down below. And Charlie? Charlie was having Fred explain to her how the *Pygmies* built the treehouse.

The party went on for a long time. At some point, Trudie plucked up some courage and started hopping around with the others. Charlie and Fred finished two bags of chips. And Willie stayed until everyone else had to go home.

CHAPTER 21

Charlie hated Sundays. Try as she might, she could not for the life of her imagine what others thought was so great about them.

Maybe it was because her mother hardly ever had Sundays off, and Grandma Stalberg was usually in a particularly foul mood on Sundays. And Charlie couldn't even meet with Freya, because she always had relatives around on Sundays. No. Sundays were unbearable. And on the Sunday before Grandma Stalberg's return, Charlie felt particularly awful.

Her mother had left very early for work. They hadn't even managed to have breakfast together. Freya was again looking after Luke, and Melanie and Trudie were never allowed out on Sundays anyway.

And so Charlie rode over to her gran's house to feed the chickens, and to erase the last traces left by the *Wild Chicks* and the *Pygmies*.

The peace party with the boys had been quite nice. Really, quite nice. The memory made this lonely Sunday even more horrid. *I'd even be happy about Fred's company right now*, Charlie thought as she pushed her bike through Grandma Stalberg's gate.

She fed the chickens, stuck her nose into Isolde's soft

feathers, and decided to put some flowers on the kitchen table for her gran. As she was cutting them, Mr. Stoutspeck's head popped over the hedge, but she just ignored him. He was the last person she wanted to talk to right now. She'd never be *that* lonely. Charlie unlocked her gran's three security locks and entered the house. She took a fresh tablecloth from the kitchen cupboard and picked a matching vase. Grandma Stalberg would probably just frown at the flowers, but she'd still be happy.

And what else? The biscuits. Of course. She could at least try to replenish the cookie tins. After all, she'd helped with the baking often enough.

Two hours later, Charlie and the floor were covered in flour. Her right thumb was burned, and one baking tray of cookies was done. Disappointed, Charlie surveyed her work. No, they really didn't look anything like Grandma Stalberg's. Never mind!

With a sigh, Charlie poured her failed attempts into the cookie tins.

"Charlie?"

Charlie spun around with a start.

Standing in the kitchen door was Freya, Luke on her arm.

"Hey!" she said, grinning. "You baked? Let's have a look."

"What are you doing here?" Charlie asked. "You gave me quite a scare. I thought my gran had come early."

Freya snickered. "Everybody's all napping at home. So I grabbed Luke and went for a walk. I thought you might be here." She put a warm cookie in Luke's hand. "They don't look like your gran's."

"I know!" said Charlie. She shrugged and poured the rest into the tin. "The thought of my gran coming back tomorrow makes me quite sick."

"Hey, look!" Freya said, looking out of the kitchen window. "There's Melanie. How did she manage to get away on a Sunday?"

Charlie grinned. "That's a first!" she mumbled. She suddenly felt like on Christmas.

"Thank god!" Melanie breathed as she entered the kitchen. "I was afraid there might be nobody here. But now the *Wild Chicks* are nearly complete, right?"

"Right," said Charlie, grinning from one ear to the next. "The only one missing is Trudie."

Melanie shook her head and plonked herself onto the kitchen sofa. "I tried to get her out, but she wasn't even at home."

"And how did you get away?" Freya asked, sitting down with Luke next to Melanie. Charlie quickly mopped up the flour from the floor and the cupboard, put the baking things away, and then sat down at the table as well.

"God!" Melanie groaned, rolling her eyes. "The chaos at my place? You have no idea. Half the family has parked itself in our couch. Two aunts, three uncles and a truckload of hideous cousins. Luckily, the boys went outside to play football and I just went with them and then made a run for it. I can't stay long, but it's better than nothing, right?"

"Better than nothing!" Freya agreed, laughing. Luke squeaked with delight and reached for Melanie's chicken feather.

"Yes? You like that, don't you?" Melanie said, tickling the little fat hand.

"How about," Charlie said excitedly, "How about I show you where we'll build our gang headquarters?"

"Great!" Melanie said with enthusiasm. "Is it far?"

Charlie shook her head. "No, just a few minutes."

"Well, what are we waiting for?" Freya said—and froze.

"What is it?" Charlie asked anxiously.

"I heard the gate," Freya said.

"Well, that definitely can't be Trudie," Melanie whispered.

Charlie turned as white as the flour still sticking to her t-shirt. "Gran," she whispered.

And then she was already in the kitchen door. Grandma Stalberg. Small, skinny, with thin lips and a strange little hat on her head. For a moment, the sight made the girls speechless. But that moment didn't last long. With a thud, Grandma Stalberg dropped her heavy travel bag.

"What's the meaning of this, Charlotte?" She was a little out of breath.

Charlie stared at her grandmother like a hypnotized rabbit. She opened her mouth, but she couldn't make a sound.

"Hello, Mrs. Stalberg!" Melanie said. "We—erm—we're friends of Charlie's."

"Well, that I already figured out for myself!" Grandma Stalberg replied brashly. "And what's that dangling from your neck? A chicken feather? Is that some kind of new fashion?"

And now Melanie was lost for words. Her face reddened and she fell silent.

"Grandma, we…" Charlie began.

"How often have I told you that I don't like strangers in my house?" her gran barked at her.

Charlie turned bright red, then white, and stared at the floor.

Then Freya got up. She squeezed Luke a little closer to give herself courage, and then went over to Grandma Stalberg.

"But we're no strangers," she said. "We are Charlie's best friends and we…" she held Luke so that he smiled directly at Grandma Stalberg, "We came by because Charlie was all alone."

Charlie's gran stared at the baby. Her lips were still tightly pressed together, but her right hand came up, as if by magic, and stroked Luke's soft baby arm.

"Is that your brother?" she asked.

Freya nodded.

"Charlie told me that you have to look after him quite often."

"It's not too often," Freya said.

Luke started babbling. He reached for Grandma Stalberg's glasses. A tiny hint of a smile crept onto her narrow lips.

"Mrs. Stalberg," Melanie got up, "We were about to leave anyway." She looked at Charlie. "Are you coming?"

Charlie shrugged, looking at her grandmother.

"What are you looking at me for?" she asked. The tiny smile had vanished. "You have to know what you're doing."

Charlie bit her lip. She looked at Freya and at Melanie, and finally she got up. "I'm coming," she said.

"Great!" said Melanie. "Goodbye, Mrs. Stalberg." And t' she quickly squeezed past Charlie's gran and ran outside.

"Yes, goodbye," Freya said, holding out her hand to Grandma Stalberg.

"Yes, yes, goodbye," she said, ignoring Freya's hand. She looked at Charlie.

"I'll be back soon," Charlie said. She walked past her gran and then turned around once more. "Didn't you want to come back tomorrow?"

"We had a fight," Grandma Stalberg said with a frown. "But that's none of your business. Dinner is at six."

"Okay," said Charlie. And then she ran through the dark corridor to the front door with Freya. Melanie was already standing outside the gate.

"You know what?" Freya whispered. She put Luke in his stroller and linked arms with Charlie. "From now on we'll meet more often, even if your gran goes blue in the face. We're a real gang now, after all."

Charlie nodded and looked over her shoulder. Her gran was standing behind the curtain, looking at them.

"Are you coming?" Melanie called over the hedge. "I don't have much time." Charlie ran to the gate. A tear rolled down her nose. Angrily, she wiped it away. Freya followed her with the stroller.

"To the *Wild Chicks!*" Charlie muttered.

"What did you say?" Freya asked.

"To the *WILD CHICKS!*" Charlie said loudly.

"Yes, to the *WILD CHICKS!*" Melanie shouted. She put her arms around the shoulders of the other two. "Who will never let anyone get them down."

"Yes, not anybody!" Charlie said. She looked back at the house once more. But Grandma Stalberg had disappeared.